C.A.

CYCLING ACROSS TIME AND SPACE

A FEMINIST BICYCLE SCIENCE FICTION AND

FANTASY ANTHOLOGY ABOUT CATS

EDITED BY

ELLY BLUE

MICROCOSM PUBLISHING

PORTLAND, OR

C.A.T.S.
CYCLING ACROSS TIME AND SPACE

Edited by Elly Blue
All content © its creators, 2021
Final editorial content © Elly Blue, 2021
This edition © Elly Blue Publishing, an imprint of Microcosm Publishing, 2021
First printing, December 10, 2021
All work remains the property of the original creators.

ISBN 9781648411199

Elly Blue Publishing, an imprint of Microcosm Publishing
2752 N Williams Ave.
Portland, OR 97227

Cover art by Cecilia Granata
Inside cover art by Paul Abbamondi
Design by Joe Biel

Thank you to Lydia Rogue for the title, cover concept, and sensitivity reading. Thank you to
David Hakas and Alana Baldwin-Joiner for their editorial assistance.

Elly Blue Publishing, an imprint of Microcosm Publishing
2752 N Williams Ave
Portland, OR 97227

This is Bikes in Space Volume 8
For more volumes visit BikesInSpace.com
For more feminist bicycle books and zines visit TakingTheLane.com

Did you know that you can buy our books directly from us at sliding scale rates? Support a small,
independent publisher and pay less than Amazon's price at www.Microcosm.Pub

To join the ranks of high-class stores that feature Microcosm titles, talk to your local rep: In
the U.S. **COMO** (Atlantic), **FUJII** (Midwest), **BOOK TRAVELERS WEST** (Pacific),
TURNAROUND (Europe), **UTP/MANDA** (Canada), **NEW SOUTH** (Australia/New
Zealand), **GPS** in Asia, Africa, India, South America, and other countries, or **FAIRE**
in the gift trade.

Library of Congress Cataloging-in-Publication Data
Names: Blue, Elly, editor.
Title: C.A.T.S. : cycling across time and space : 11 feminist science
    fiction and fantasy stories about bicycling and cats / edited by Elly
    Blue.
Other titles: Cats
Description: Portland, OR : Microcosm Publishing, [2021] | Series: Bikes in
    space ; Vol. 8 | Summary: "Has your cat been plotting to take over
    command of your spaceship? This and other important questions are
    tackled in the 11 science fiction and fantasy stories in this volume,
    told variously from the perspectives of humans and cats. A bicycle
    designer finds an exciting new technical challenge on a planet inhabited
    by felines. A wise cat tries to convince an excited puppy not to chase
    cyclists. On Mars, a cat helps save the life of their human after a
    quake. In other stories, a student must live with the consequences of
    magic gone awry, a cat contrives to go on a bicycle trip, a police robot
    learns empathy, a captured tiger lashes out, and a young sphinx finds
    her wings. Featuring stories by Alice Dryden, Cherise Fong, Gerri Leen,
    Gretchin Lair, Jessie Kwak, Judy Upton, Juliet Wilson, Kathleen Jowitt,
    Kiya Nicoll, Monique Cuillerier, and Summer Jewel Keown"-- Provided by
    publisher.
Identifiers: LCCN 2021033369 | ISBN 9781648411199 (trade paperback)
Subjects: LCSH: Science fiction, American. | Feminist fiction, American. |
    Cycling--Fiction. | Cats--Fiction.
Classification: LCC PS648.S3 C325 2021 | DDC 813/.087620806--dc23
LC record available at https://lccn.loc.gov/2021033369

[TABLE OF CONTENTS]

INTRODUCTION

I n 1963, Valentina Tereshkova became the first human woman to travel to space. A Russian textile worker, she was selected for the space program because of her love of amateur skydiving; the Soviets were determined to beat the U.S. in sending a woman to space and scoured the country's parachutist clubs for candidates.

That same year, a French catstronaut named Félicette became the first cat to go to space, and to this day is the only feline to have survived spaceflight. She trained much as human astronauts do, with centrifugal force simulating the gravity of re-entry, practice being confined in a small space, and the simulated noise of rockets. She didn't long survive her return to Earth; to add further indignity, she has often been mistakenly commemorated on postage stamps as "Felix." The error speaks for itself.

Tereshkova has fared much better, going on to become an engineer and career politician as well as an international celebrity. After her rush into orbit, it was almost 20 years before another woman went to space. She remains the only woman to have been on a solo mission in space.

With these early cosmonauts in mind, here is the eight volume of the Bikes in Space series of feminist science fiction (with a good deal of fantasy in the mix).

What makes the Bikes in Space books feminist? I get asked this question frequently, especially when our calls for submissions are open. More amusing is when people don't ask, but assume—

my favorite example was someone who mused, "So you publish stories about planets with no men? No, I get it—all the men are enslaved!" More frequent is the assumption that all the stories must by written by women in order to be feminist, or that the stories need to be overtly about fighting sexism.

None of that's quite right. When I first started editing this series, I had one simple rule—it would not include stories that were overtly sexist. That includes stories that glorify gendered or sexual violence, tedious stereotypes like strong men saving wilting women or strong women portrayed as militantly anti-man, casual slurs, or anything told un-self-reflexively through the male gaze. Which seems like a pretty easy and obvious bar, but I still get plenty of submissions for every volume that don't meet it. Over time, that bar has stayed pretty much the same, and I've learned to steer clear of stories with racist or transphobic themes and dog whistles as well.

There has been one key addition to my criteria, though, something that all the stories must be rather than must not be. In a word, it's agency.

The idea of agency had been building in my mind—and story selections—for a while. This is the eighth volume of Bikes in Space; while editing the fourth (*Biketopia*), I was a little chagrined to figure out that the strongest stories in each volume were ones where the protagonist is faced with a meaningful choice, takes a risk, and is transformed. Seems basic, but I came around to it the hard way. (And when I did, it made me a better editor of nonfiction, too.) No amount of gorgeous scenery, sparkling dialogue, smooth pacing, or clever devices can save a story that's missing that key element, because without it there is no story. Since then, I've learned to look for this element in screening submissions for these books.

A few years later, I was on a cross-country train ride, reading the new edition of the 1990s book *Jane*, which recounts the story of the Chicago Abortion Project and the team of women who worked outside the law to organize affordable, shame-free abortions in the years leading up to Roe v. Wade. Their story is moving and heroic, but what stuck with me most was the reason they did it, and which imbued every aspect of their operation: they were fighting for our right to have agency over our bodies and lives. At every step of the process, they asked the patients who came to them to deeply consider what they wanted, and encouraged them to choose freely, regardless of the coercions or obligations (whether that was to commit to the pregnancy or have the abortion) being put on them from families, partners, and society. "Choice" was never a euphemism for abortion—it was a call to each person to take full responsibility for their own thoughts, feelings, and decisions, even as external forces were doing their best to strip those powers away.

At the time, this was revolutionary—possession of a uterus greatly reduced your economic power and legal protections—and today when some of us can take a little more equality for granted, it's no less of a revelation. At least, looking out those train windows and contemplating the moments in my life that I've defaulted to passivity, it was to me. Agency, I decided, is the key element in feminism, or any other liberation movement in which we are fighting to be able to live our lives as fully human, fully adult. This gave me the language that is what continues to motivate this project and attempt to do it better every time—as well as all the others I work on, including nonfiction.

Around that same time, I was starting to read more science fiction and fantasy with an editors' eye. "What is the fantasy?" I wondered about each book (of any genre, nonfiction included), and the answer often surprised me. One pervasive trope I started to notice in fiction written with ostensibly strong female leads is a love story that begins with one partner (almost always a man) kidnapping another (almost always a woman). Seeing this once, I began to see it everywhere. This fantasy depicts the opposite of agency; many fictional women have valiantly fought their way free of truly hopeless situations, only to return (albeit, in the best of them, with a lot of spirited, boundary-setting dialogue) to the arms of the person who made it necessary for them to fight those battles to begin with. Very occasionally the would-be kidnapper even demonstrates their remorse through changed behavior; in most, it turns out to all have been a big misunderstanding, and nobody's learned a thing. But we can learn from it; once we can see it, we don't have to repeat this depressing theme in fiction or in life.

This obsession with agency absolutely came out in the story selections for this book. The characters shown here are positively brimming with agency, gumption, and a can-do attitude. And I was tickled to receive so many good stories featuring cats as the protagonists, many of which made it into this volume. After all, if anyone knows about making their own choices, cats do.

I hope you enjoy these stories. As I write this introduction, the COVID-19 pandemic is still ravaging the US and a violent right wing insurrection is simmering, but these stories were all written over a year ago, before any of the plot twists of the 2020s came to pass. Perhaps by the time you pick up this book, reading about characters eating in restaurants and having animated conversations with unmasked strangers won't feel just as far fetched as the stories about cats living on spaceships. The future seems as uncertain now as it ever has, but it will absolutely be what we make it.

Elly Blue
Portland, Oregon
January, 2021

MYX SENDS IT

Jessie Kwak

*I*f I don't move, she can't see me.

Myx crouches, still as stone, fighting her tail's urge to flick back and forth in terror. She's pretty sure that the creatures can only see movement — it's always worked before. Of course, before, they've always been flying past her with magical, wingless speed.

They don't have wings, but they do have their two-wheeled contraptions. And that seems to be enough.

Myx has been fascinated by the creatures since she first glimpsed one soaring bright and colorful, smearing rainbow hues she doesn't even have names for against the brown and green backdrop of her forest home. They fly single file in formation, yelling back and forth to each other — *braaap! braaap!* — like Canada geese soaring overhead in their migratory patterns.

Myx doesn't think the creatures are migrating, because she sees the same ones over and over. They seem to stay in distinct groups, maybe flying together with their litter? In fact, she has seen a few juveniles, wee ones teetering along the trails on two wheels at the encouragement of their parents.

This one — a female — has gotten separated from her flock. At first, Myx was worried about her, but she doesn't seem to be lost. Merely resting.

Myx was resting, too. She's been trying to fly all morning and now she's exhausted, but too embarrassed to go back to the den. When she goes back, her brothers and sisters will probably have all mastered flight. They'll ask her how she did. They'll show off their swoops.

She can't bear to tell them that she *still* hasn't figured out how to fly.

The two-wheeled creature takes a swig from a cylindrical fruit she detaches from her contraption. Her gaze swings past Myx, who lets out a quick breath of relief.

It's true.

If I don't move, she can't —

Myx's breath disturbs a leaf, which tickles her whiskers. She sneezes.

Oh, no.

"Oh my gosh."

The creature stares straight at her, wide-eyed in shock and wonder. Myx stares back. She's frozen in terror.

"What *are* you?" The girl leans forward, tipping precariously on her two wheeled contraption in order to get a better look at Myx. She carefully unclips the sack on her back and opens it, trying to find something without taking her eyes off of Myx. She swears under her breath, then glances down to find what she's looking for.

Without the girl's eyes on her, Myx finds she can move again. She instinctively flaps her wings, hoping this time she'll soar majestically into the air like her mother — but she gains only the most pathetic bit of lift. It's just enough that when she leaps it takes her a little bit farther than usual — though nothing impressive. Myx lands on a tree trunk with claws out, then scrambles up the tree to crouch in the crook of a branch, heart thudding in her chest.

The creature looks up, fist closed around a flat, square stone. Her shoulders slump when she sees the empty rock where Myx had been crouched, then she straightens and cranes her neck, looking for Myx.

She had originally stopped off to the side of the trail, but in her distraction she's now standing in the middle of it. And another one of the creatures is barreling around the corner.

For a horrible second, Myx thinks the second creature will run into the first one. She lets out a screech of warning, just as the second creature yells and skids to a stop in a cloud of dust and gravel.

"Sorry!" the girl yells.

"Are you all right?" the boy asks.

"I just thought I saw something," the girl says. "Like a ... like a cat."

"A house cat?"

The girl shakes her head. "No, more like a tiny lion. But with … just kind of like a tiny lion."

The boy's eyes go wide. "A mountain lion?"

"No, it was small." The girl cups her hands in front of her, fingers spread like she's cradling a creature the size of Myx.

"A *baby* mountain lion? We definitely need to get out of here. C'mon."

"I'll follow you." The girl gets back in position on her two wheeled contraption as the boy speeds off, but she doesn't fly away yet. She scans the forest once more, eyes narrowed. "You're like a tiny lion, but you had wings. I know you did."

And she's gone.

Myx crouches trembling in the tree branch, shaken by the encounter — though the heady mix of terror and excitement is slowly fading as she plays the girl's words over and over in her head.

Myx may have wings, but she certainly can't do anything with them.

She picks her way slowly down the trunk of the tree, tail drooping.

Back at the den, it's just as she's been picturing. Her brothers and sisters have all seemed to master their fledgling wings and they're soaring around the den while Myx's mother looks on proudly. Myx's mother greets her with the nuzzle and licks her behind the ear.

"How was your practice?" she asks.

"It was great," Myx lies. "I totally got it."

"That's wonderful! Will you show me?"

Myx arches back, stretching her paws out in front of her. "I think I wore myself out," she says. She doesn't quite meet her mother's golden eyes. "I'm just gonna take a little nap."

She pads inside the den and tucks her paws under her chin, curling her tail around her nose. She scrunches her eyes closed, trying to block out the sounds of her siblings's jubilant shouts as they soar around the mouth of the den.

If she can't see them, they're not all flying without her.

.   .   .

Myx has worn herself out again by lunch, but she is determined not to go home a second time without learning how to fly. She took a small break to watch the creatures soar by, jealous, and now she's ready for another round. She leaps, tumbles. Leaps, tumbles.

Leaps, *tumb* —

Myx lands poorly on the edge of a crumbly dirt cutaway and rolls down tail over ears. She lands in a jumble on hard-packed dirt, twigs and leaf debris clinging to her fur.

She gets to her feet with a furious yowl.

Myx has to be the only sphinx in the history of the world who can't land on her feet. All the older members of their little pride have told her this with a hint of amusement, like the fact that Myx is so klutzy is the cutest thing they've ever seen. Myx doesn't want to be adorable. She wants to be graceful. She wants to fly, and she wants to do it *today*.

She growls at her stupid, clumsy wings like that will make them finally work right, so caught up in her frustrations that she doesn't realize she's standing in the middle of one of the trails the creatures use for their own flights. Not until she hears the telltale *zzzzzzzzz!*

Myx leaps at the short cliff she just tumbled down, flapping her wings with all her might but only getting the barest amount of lift. It's not enough. Her claws dig into the soft, crumbly earth and she can't get purchase. She scrambles, panicking, and her claw catches in an exposed root just as one of the creatures rolls around the corner.

Myx freezes.

The creature sees her.

It's the same girl as the day before, though she's changed her plumage into something equally bright and glorious, the color of berries and sunsets. She's going slower than the creatures normally go. She seems tired; she's dusty and covered in dirt and twigs, too.

Maybe they're both having a bad day.

The girl's eyes go wide. "It's you!" She slowly, carefully lays her contraption down off the side of the trail and digs into the sack on her back once more. Myx flaps her wings miserably and scrabbles at the dirt cliff. Her claw refuses to budge from the root.

The girl pulls her thin square stone out of her sack and holds it up in front of her face. Myx mewls, scared and exhausted, and the girl's expression turns from wonder to concern.

"Are you trapped? Oh, you poor thing. It's okay, little buddy. I won't hurt you."

She puts her stone in her pocket, then takes a few careful steps across the trail until she's close enough to Myx that she can reach out and touch her. She cradles her carefully in one palm while she uses her long fingers to unhook Myx's claw from the root. Myx freezes in her hands, trembling, not sure what the girl will do with her. But the girl just sets her on the trail as gently as possible.

"There you go."

Myx hears it at the same time as the girl does — another creature is barreling around the corner. The girl jumps off the trail with a yell, and in a moment of panic, Myx scrambles after her and cowers under her two wheeled contraption.

There's a terrifying skid sound of wheels on gravel, and the second creature yells as he flies by. "You okay?"

"Just taking a break!" the girl yells back.

"Braaaap!!" the boy calls, indicating his position to the rest of the flock.

The girl sighs, shaking her head in wonder, then reaches down for her contraption. Her eyes widened as she sees Myx crouched beneath it.

"You're still here!" She reaches for the stone in her pocket and holds it up in front of her again, and Myx bunches her muscles to run. The girl stops. "It's okay, fine. No pictures."

Myx wonders what pictures are as the girl places the stone back in her sack.

"No one's ever gonna believe me."

She holds out her hand, her fingers stopping shy of Myx's nose. Myx already has sat in that hand, and she knows the girl is gentle, though she doesn't know much else about these creatures.

Except that they can fly.

Myx sniffs the girls fingertips, then licks her rough tongue across her palm in thanks for rescuing her. The girl laughs and shivers. "That tickles." She looks sadly over her shoulder. "I should get going — they'll be wondering what happened to me. It was nice to meet you, whatever you are."

The girl's going to fly away, leaving Myx here with her own useless wings.

Myx mewls at her; she's starting to have an idea.

When the girl stands and mounts her contraption once more, Myx trots up to her, rubbing her cheek, then her shoulder against the girl's ankle.

"Aw, you're such a sweet … kitty thing." The girl reaches down to scratch Myx's ears — it feels marvelous — and Myx puts her paws on the girl's knee, stretching to her full height. After a moment's hesitation, the girl reaches down to scoop her up. Myx climbs up the girl's shoulder, trying not to let her claws snag in the fine material of the girl's plumage, until she's nestled on the top of the sack the girl wears. It makes a perfect perch.

The girl laughs. "You want to go for a ride? Well, I'm sorry I won't be very fast, I crashed in that gnarly root section back there. But I'll see what I can do."

The girl takes off, hesitant at first, then with more confidence as Myx holds tight, claws digging into the sack.

It's amazing.

They soar over rollers and swoop around turns. Once they bounce down a set of roots — that's terrifying — but when Myx screeches in fear, the girl stays on smoother parts of the trail. She picks up speed as they go, soaring with glorious abandon.

So this is what it feels like.

Myx tentatively spreads her wings, testing the way the wind feels under her feathers, and for a second she gets actual lift. Oh!

Oh.

That makes sense. Something about the angle — she's been going about this wrong. If she holds her wings like this —

Myx's claws are the only thing that hold her to the girl's sack, and she quickly draws her wings back in, nervous at what she almost did.

But?

What she almost did was flying. Really flying.

Myx takes a deep breath, purrs a thank you at the girl, retracts her claws, and spreads her wings.

She soars.

For a minute, she follows along the girl's bright plumage below, before she begins to worry about how far she's gone. She should head back to the den.

Myx flaps her wings, a little unsteady on the turn, but she doesn't fall.

She's flying.

She can't wait to show the others.

MISS TOMKINS TAKES A HOLIDAY

Kathleen Jowitt

I was in a cheerful mood that morning; I had been so, in fact, for the last several days, ever since the management at Flatwood's had agreed to the workers' demands and the strike had been called off. Cheerful, yes, and ready to turn my hand to the next task.

It was with some surprise, then, that I heard my superior say, "You should take a holiday."

"But I can't possibly," I said. "There's so much work to be done."

"Others can do it."

"Why should they, when I'm here and willing?"

"Miss Tomkins, I mean it." Mrs. Graves' face was serious. "You should take a holiday. Very soon."

There was something about her expression that impressed me. "Why do you say that?"

She removed her spectacles and, while she wiped them, said, "We have heard worrying news about Flatwood's."

"But the board agreed that the workers' demands were reasonable."

"The board as a body, yes. Not all the individual members of the board." Mrs. Graves leaned forward, "I received a message from Mr. Aubrey Cannon. He was very anxious that I should impress upon you the danger of crossing Lord Howe. He suggested that I familiarize myself with the news regarding the Honourable Antonia Sanderson if I anticipated any difficulty in persuading you." She touched a newspaper clipping on her desk.

I resisted the urge to glance at it. I knew the story. "Sanderson... the lady who had oil of vitriol thrown in her face."

"Precisely. I don't know whether you are aware that she had recently broken off her engagement to Lord Howe. I had not made the connection. Mr. Cannon made it for me, rather forcibly. He struck me, Miss Tomkins, as a young man who was very worried."

"I see," I said. I felt sure that Mrs. Graves' concern was unfounded, but nevertheless I was shaken by the conviction with which she spoke. "Perhaps it *is* time I took a holiday. Where do you think might be pleasant at this time of year?"

"I always like the seaside." Mrs. Graves looked distinctly relieved. "I fear you might find it dull, though."

"I think," I said, "that perhaps I shall make a cycling tour.'"

I would not go so far as to imply that I had my pannier bags packed and ready for just such an eventuality, but it was certainly true that I had spent many a winter evening with an Ordnance Survey map spread out on the rug, planning the trips that I had never yet found the leisure to undertake. Now the leisure was being pressed upon me. It took me perhaps half an hour to gather together the necessities. But I was not yet ready to leave.

I made my way along the corridor with a mind to asking one of my neighbours to feed Aster, my cat, and here fate intervened. Not one of them answered my knock at their door. I was certain that I had heard the front door open and close at least twice while I was packing, and that I'd heard footsteps on the stairs after that, so they couldn't all have gone out, but for all the response I got I might have been a ghost.

Mrs. Morland's stuffed owl glared down at me. I glared back at it.

I felt a warm, insistent pressure against my ankles. "I'm trying to sort out your lodgings, puss-cat," I said to Aster. I supposed that if worse came to worst, I could take her with me.

She rubbed herself against my legs and purred.

I continued down the corridor to Mrs. Morland's door and wasn't altogether surprised when she, too, failed to answer my knock. Well, I thought, I was up to date with my rent and it was hardly her business if I chose to take a holiday. I returned to my room to write her a note.

I knocked at all the doors again on my way out, but again, no one one answered.

"Well," I said, "what shall we do? I can't very well leave you here with no notice." Aster leapt up into the basket on the front of my bicycle and curled herself up in it. I laughed, and went to find the basket lid and the leather straps that held it down.

As far from my mind as the thought of a holiday had been when I woke, now that I was obliged to take one, the idea had its attractions. It was not quite eleven o'clock on a fine May morning with just enough briskness to the air to stop the sunshine from being oppressively warm. I relished the thought of a jaunt into the countryside.

I mounted the bicycle and struck out westward. At first, it was no different from any other day: streets of smoky houses, the bustle of trams and carts, and women scrubbing doorsteps. But gradually, the houses became newer and less cramped, and young green trees lined the pavements.

·   ·   ·

Half an hour later, I could fairly say that I was in the country. I pedalled on, and the frisson of fear and the bustle of departure gave way once again to the cheerful mood with which I had begun the day.

I stopped at a village bakery to buy myself a bun for lunch and at the fishmonger's for something for Aster, and cycled on a little further beyond the limit of the houses before stopping under a shady tree. When I unfastened the basket, Aster uncurled herself and raised the front half of her body to look over the edge. Apparently liking what she saw, she put two paws on the rim, pulled herself over, and poured herself to the ground.

It didn't occur to me then or at any other time to worry about her running away. Ever since I'd returned from my meeting with Mrs. Graves, she'd stuck so closely to my heels that she might as well have said out loud, "Go where you like: I'm coming with you."

Now she crouched at my side, eating her fish while I sat and ate my bun and swigged at my flask of tea. It wasn't very ladylike, but the holiday mood prevailed and I didn't care.

It was very pleasant under my shady tree and the afternoon was warm. Reclining on my elbow to read the newspaper I'd brought with me, I soon found the print blurring into dappled sunlight and fell asleep.

And I dreamed—though I could not now tell you what I dreamed of. I can recall only a sense of claustrophobia, of being trapped in a small, dark space, with something formless and unspeakable outside it, something that came closer and closer. I dared not escape—and yet I knew I must.

There was a sound of snarling.

And suddenly the dream changed, and I was walking next to a cold, breathlessly beautiful brook somewhere in the high mountains, through a meadow starred with tiny and exquisite flowers.

When I woke, the sun had moved some considerable way towards the west, and Aster was curled in the crook of my elbow. My watch had stopped, but the chimes of the church clock drifted over the fields. Three slow strokes followed. It was time I was on my way. I was alarmed to see footmarks in the dust and, chiding myself for my carelessness, I hurried to make sure that my bicycle had not been tampered with. But all was in order.

There were other footprints beyond my own and the unknown intruders'. Not human ones, though. They belonged to some good-sized mammal: a fox, I thought, or perhaps a badger. Town-bred, I was no expert in these matters.

I mounted my bicycle once more and rode on. It was some time later that it struck me that those marks had seemed just as fresh as my own. I told myself that I could not possibly be sure of that and kept on for another two hours through the lengthening afternoon before I came to the first of the three villages that I had noted as possibilities for an overnight stay.

It was a sleepy little place with a cluster of cottages around the church and a pub that I thought it best not to enter. But there was a larger house, set back a little way from the road, with a discreet notice that read *The Willows: VACANCIES*. It would do very nicely.

The door was opened by a woman in her late twenties, harassed-looking but pleasant. She was dismayed, either by the bicycle, by Aster, or perhaps simply by my dishevelled appearance after a day on the road, but she hid it well and showed me a shed where I could lock the bicycle up for the night. I assured her that Aster was house-trained and she let me take her inside. She told me that it was no trouble at all to arrange a bowl of soup and she carried a jug of hot water up to my bedroom so that I could wash. I suspected that she would be making the soup herself. I had seen no other human being around the place, although from time to time I heard a querulous *"Elsie!"*, presumably directed at my companion.

·   ·   ·

Elsie showed me into the dining room—spotless, but chilly even on this spring day—and brought me not only soup, but a plate of ham, new potatoes, and vegetables.

When she came to clear the plates, I asked her whether she had any help.

I talk to a fair few young women in my line of work. Older women, too, and some men, but, things being as they are these days, much of the workforce is female and under the age of twenty-five. They have enough self-respect to have declined a life of drudgery in domestic service and most of them have fire enough to resist exploitation in the factories and workshops where I meet them—if one can but kindle that fire!

I said that I talk to them. Perhaps it would be more accurate to say that I listen to them. They know, better than I, what's wrong in those places where they're employed, and often they know, better than I, how it can be mended; and if I let them talk, they very often hit on it. All I do is ask a question or so, occasionally correct some misapprehension.

This was how it was with Elsie. My casual inquiry and sympathetic expression were enough to prompt the whole story.

"Well, you see, Mother runs this whole place on her own, and I don't like to think what she'd do without me... She'd have to pay somebody, you see, and she couldn't possibly afford to pay them enough to do all the work that needs doing."

I nodded.

"And I know what you're going to say, that I oughtn't to think about that, that I owe her my loyalty and my help and..."

"Oh, no," I said, "I wasn't going to say that at all."

"Edward—a friend—says that I ought to leave her to it."

"And would you like to?"

"It would feel like a failure, somehow." She shook her head. "But sometimes, I think I'm past caring about that."

"What do you suppose your mother would do if you weren't here?" I asked. "Suppose you went under a bus?"

For the first time, she smiled. "There isn't much chance of that around here. You see the bus coming a mile away, and there are only three a day."

"Imagine you didn't see one coming."

She bit her lip. "She'd have to sell up, I suppose."

"And if she were to become too infirm to keep running the place even with the substantial amount of help that you give her?" I held my finger up to dissuade her from arguing. "Would you want to take it over?"

"Don't talk like that," she said mechanically. A flush rose at her cheekbones.

"I apologize. But sooner or later it must come to that, you know."

She nodded helplessly. "I know. And no, I'd be glad to see the back of the whole enterprise. But you see, that's the thing. She isn't as well as she used to be, so I feel it's my duty to help her for as long as possible. You don't know," she added, "how often I've said to myself, just *go*, marry Edward, and leave her to manage as best she can."

"And yet you haven't."

"I wouldn't know where to start."

I raised my eyebrows. "Oh?"

"How to tell her. Whether she would be willing to sell the house and where she would go if she did. What everyone would *say*..." She frowned, angry with herself. "I apologize. I ought not to burden you with my private frustrations."

"Not at all," I said. "I did ask. You say you don't know what people will say?"

"No. I do. They'd say, *So she's caught him at last*, or, which would be worse, *So she's left her poor mother to struggle on alone*, or..."

"Or?" I prompted.

"Or, worst of all, *So she's finally got away from the old hag.*"

The potential melodrama of the moment was punctured by an inquisitive *miaow?* Elsie laughed and absently bent to stroke Aster. "Of course," she said, "the obvious thing to do would be for both of us to leave this place. Edward's always talking about going south and painting. Painting what he wants to, I mean. I'd like that. And

Mother could go to some seaside resort and make herself the life and soul of the place. If we sold this house, it would keep all of us for years..." Aster was purring now.

"It sounds wonderful," I said.

She smiled. "It does, doesn't it? Well, one never knows. Perhaps I shall."

I slept soundly that night. For all I know Elsie might never have gone to bed, but she knocked at my door in a much more cheerful state in the morning. Our conversation was variously practical and trivial: I sensed that returning to the concerns we had discussed the previous evening would not help to resolve them any faster. I must be content, I suspected, without knowing how she would make her situation tolerable. I was confident that she would.

A little gang of children gathered to watch over the fence as I pumped up the tires and oiled the chain of my bicycle. I was conscious of them muttering and giggling behind me. Aster washed her paws disdainfully.

I finished my preparations, straightened up, and wiped my hands on a bit of rag. Prompted by a whisper of "Go *on*, Bertie," the tallest of the boys stepped forward and asked, with a bold but embarrassed grin, "Are you a witch, miss?"

I raised my eyebrows. "Well," I said, "do you think every woman who travels alone with a cat is a witch? And did you ever hear of a witch traveling by bicycle?"

This seemed to confuse them; they backed off a few paces and resumed their *sotto voce* conference. One of the girls came forward and said, "No, we didn't. But that doesn't mean they don't ever."

I laughed and acknowledged the logic of her point. "But," I said, "do you think I'd tell you if I were?"

This divided the group: some seemed to see it as a clear admission of guilt, others, as a mere bagatelle. I strapped my bags down to the rack, picked up Aster and put her in the basket, and, with a cheery wave, left them to their debate.

·   ·   ·

Some while after two o'clock, I rolled into a large village of conspicuous gentility. I was hot, hungry, and thirsty, and I stopped with some relief at a place that advertised *TEAS*. Having let Aster out and locked my bicycle to a lamp post that I would be able to see from the window, I shook the dust from my clothes as best I could and entered the building.

The proprietor looked disposed to make trouble about Aster, but my clever black cat was too quick for her, taking two prim steps forward and looking up at her with a disarming mew. The woman's face cleared as if by magic; she squatted down to scratch Aster's head, and then, straightening up, said civilly, "Table for one, madam? And I'm sure I can find a bit of fish for the cat."

"That's very kind of you," I said.

She seated me at a table and left with Aster at her heels. A girl of about twenty-one appeared to take my order, a depressed, tired-looking creature for whom, judging by the sigh with which she put it down, a teapot was an intolerable burden. She held herself stiffly, as if she was trying to compress herself so as to occupy the smallest possible area of floor space.

I smiled at her as she placed a plate of sandwiches next to the teacup. "Thank you," I said. "What's your name?"

"It's Mary, madam. Mary Fletcher." She glanced around as if fearful that she had betrayed some state secret. It was more than depression and fatigue, I decided: she was scared.

"Well, thank you, Mary." I wondered what it was that she was scared of. "Have you worked here long?"

"Since I left school, madam."

Seven years, then, at a guess. What kept her here? "Do you enjoy your work?"

She said, "Yes, madam," but her tone was so bleak that I knew it for a lie. I kept silent, smiling slightly, until she added, "It's a job, isn't it?"

"Only a job?"

She flushed. "What more could I expect? I've been lucky, everyone says, after..."

Asking *After what?* would have got me nowhere, so instead I said, "Everyone?"

"Well, Mrs. Dunn. And *him*." She glanced around the room once again, as if expecting *him* to be lurking behind the chintz curtains.

"Mr. Dunn?" I guessed.

She shook her head, "Mr. Crabb. Her brother."

"Awkward, is he?" She didn't reply, but her face told me. "Does she *know*?" I asked.

"About my trouble? Yes."

"I mean, does she know about him? Have you told her?"

"What would be the point? She'd just think I was leading him on." She looked at me pleadingly. "I swear I'm not."

"I'm sure you're not," I said. I frowned. This situation was clearly intolerable, with the man making a nuisance of himself, but it would be folly for Mary to leave without securing a favorable reference, which would not be forthcoming if she were to disclose her true motive for leaving. And she was obviously haunted by the remembrance of the events that had led to her seeking out this uncertain sanctuary in the first place: she could not be expected to up and leave without any idea of where she might go next, or how she might support herself if she got there. This was a situation that called for the exertion of less subtle persuasion.

That would be a conversation with Mrs. Dunn and, seeing how quickly she had taken to Aster, I felt confident that I could persuade her that it was in her interests to give Mary a good reference. But that would be of no use until Mary herself felt secure in her ability to make something of it. So I said, as if I were changing the subject, "What would you like to do, if you had the choice? Where would you like to work?"

She glanced around the room once more, and I wondered if I had pushed too hard. But she said, "Somewhere I didn't have to be on my feet all day. Somewhere I didn't have to be polite to customers."

There was a flash of something defiant in her eyes, and I was glad to see it though it was directed at me. She would do, I thought; she would do very well.

I complimented Mrs. Dunn on a delicious spread and her well-trained and well-mannered staff, and introduced the idea that sooner or later, Mary would naturally want to move on, and that it would be a kindness to enable her to move beyond the limitations, whatever they might have been, of her early life.

Aster was purring loudly and looking very pleased with herself. Mrs. Dunn seemed cautiously receptive. I judged discretion to be the better part of valor and left things there, letting her ask me about the purpose of my journey. I told her about a fictitious sister with whom I planned to stay that evening, which allowed me to introduce a deceased and equally fictitious brother-in-law who had caused a good deal of trouble with the maids.

"And do you know," I said, "she didn't find out why she couldn't keep any of them until he... insulted the vicar's daughter. It was a terrible scandal, and while I hate to say it was a mercy that he passed on when he did, she had to move away, and of course she hasn't had any trouble since... Anyway, I mustn't bore you with my family woes, and I must be on my way. Thank you so much— this has been a delightful interlude."

I left her looking rather thoughtful. Perhaps, I thought, I would take tea there again on my way home.

In the meantime, however, I had some miles to go before the next settlement that looked as if it might be large enough to have a respectable overnight lodging, and it was already well past four o'clock. My average speed that afternoon was considerably greater than the leisurely trundle I'd been managing over the preceding legs.

I passed through a few hamlets, overgrown farms, really, which promised and offered nothing in the way of a bed. I considered the possibility of sleeping in a haystack, but it was not the season for such things, and besides, I was of an age to consider linen and feathers distinctly appealing.

In the next village the pub was boarded up; I didn't stop to inquire why. But in the village after that, the Goat and Compasses turned out to be clean and hospitable, and Mrs. Lewis, the landlady, prepared to cater for cat and bicycle alike, if I "didn't mind having the animal in my room." I did not mind at all.

I washed and, finding myself unaccountably restless despite the miles I had cycled that day, went out for a brisk walk around the village. Aster followed me. It was when I had almost completed my circuit of the four streets on which all the buildings of significance were situated that I saw a young man, flaxen-haired, dressed expensively but not ostentatiously. And he saw me.

I could not suppress a start of recognition. I knew that face, had seen it sneering across a boardroom table when I had accompanied Florrie Seward as she put the workers' case to the management.

And Lord Howe knew me, there was no doubt of that. He raised his hat to me with what might have been taken for courtesy—but I saw the expression in his eyes.

At my feet, Aster hissed, and the fur on her tail stood up like a bottlebrush.

I nodded, and he passed on by. I remained where I stood, facing in the opposite direction until the sound of his footsteps had faded away. I did not want him to think that he had rattled me, nor did I want him to know where I was staying—although it would not, of course, have been a difficult guess.

I wondered whether I ought to move on, but it was getting late, and a look at the map showed me that the next village—barely more than a hamlet—was at least another hour's ride. It told me, too, that I ought not have been surprised by Lord Howe's presence: we were a scant mile away from Gossington House, the family seat. Why had I not struck south for the Downs, or into Essex, instead? But it was too late for regrets. I would simply have to keep out of his way and leave as early as possible in the morning.

With that thin comfort in mind, I returned to the Goat and Compasses and ate the supper that Mrs. Lewis had kept for me. Then I retired to my room for the evening.

The air was close, and I wondered if there was a thunderstorm on the way. Even my light nightgown felt uncomfortably warm. I lay beneath a single sheet and listened to the noises of the night.

Eventually, I must have dozed off, for once again I was caught in the dream of a confined space and an unseen foe outside it. Now it was connected in my mind with the idea of Lord Howe. I seemed to see his angel-face peering down at me from the roof of my prison, a sneer on his lips. I shook my fist at him, but he, knowing that I ran from him, only laughed.

I began to search for a door, a window, some way out. I tried to scale the featureless walls to reach the hatch where that mocking face still hovered. It was useless.

Up until now, the dream had been silent, but then there came a low growl, rising slowly and terribly in volume until it was a roar. All of a sudden, silence rushed back in. And a reply came in the form of a high, horrible, human cry.

Whether it was this that woke me, or the first clap of thunder, I don't know. I sat up in bed. The first few raindrops were spattering on the window. I supposed that I ought to close it, but I could not have moved from that bed for all the powers in creation, and there was nothing below the window that would spoil.

I called, "Aster! Aster!" in a low voice, but she did not come to me. A depression in the covers at my feet showed where she had been curled up, but it was cold. She had been gone some time.

Greatly perturbed, I lay down again and watched the harsh brilliance of the lightning reflected across the ceiling and listened to the thunder, until the storm passed and the rain smoothed itself into one soothing thrum...

·   ·   ·

When I woke again, the rain had stopped. In the corner of the room, Aster crunched peaceably at the bones of some small animal. Hoping absently that she would not leave too much of a mess behind, I turned over and went back to sleep.

I slept rather later than I had meant to. My host brought me breakfast herself—for, as I was to see, the sheer pleasure of telling me the news when she did so.

"Dreadful news this morning, Miss Tomkins. Poor Lord Howe," her face showed little sympathy, "attacked by some wild beast last night."

"A wild beast? What do you mean?"

"Some sort of tiger, or panther, from the marks on his face. Or that was what Major Cadwallader said it must be, judging by what Bates told him."

"But how extraordinary," I said, and noticed that my tea slopped very slightly in the cup. "Where can it have come from?"

She shook her head. "Escaped from a zoo or circus, no doubt." Evidently, there was no creature of local folklore to be invoked.

"Good heavens. Was Lord Howe badly hurt?"

"It won't kill him," Mrs. Lewis said, "but it will spoil his looks, and keep him quiet for a month or so."

I thought of Antonia Sanderson, and I could not bring myself to be sorry for Lord Howe. Nor, judging by her expression, could Mrs. Lewis. I wondered what sort of landlord he made. "In that case," I said, "I trust that he'll find the experience improving."

"We can only hope so." She cleared her throat.

"Well," I said to myself when she had left the room, "I suppose there's nothing to stop me going home now." I thought of the correspondence that must be piling up for me on my desk, of how Mrs. Graves would look up when I came into the office and say, "Miss Tomkins! *Just* the person!" I thought of the trouble that was brewing at Mackay's works. And I could not bring myself to care very much about any of it. Surely, I admonished myself, I was not frightened? Lord Howe was an exception—an extremely unpleasant one, but an exception nonetheless.

I knew it was not fear.

Aster purred and rubbed herself against my legs. I bent to stroke her.

"On the other hand," I said to myself, "when I spend my days agitating for the rights of others to claim the recreation time that is so important to their health and well-being, can I in good conscience deny that same leisure to myself? Perhaps I ought not to."

And Aster purred louder still.

MIND THE TIGER PLUME

Cherise Fong

"It's so small. Must be a house cat from Earth."

"Doesn't look like a kitten."

"Wonder if it talks?"

"Leave it alone for now. It'll come out when it's ready."

I opened my eyes. Everything was blurry, bright, blinding white. Slowly, the landscape extending before me came into focus: ice. Vast plains of glistening crystals gradually fading into shadowy dunes and jagged craters under a jade green sky. I spotted two silhouettes in the distance, feline figures with long curled tails and pointed ears, moving gracefully above the frozen floor. Were they flying?

I opened my mouth to call out, but before I could make a sound the entire landscape blurred again. Then I remembered where I was. The window had steamed up in front of me. I was still inside the capsule where Cass had left me, launched alone into outer space, who knows how long ago.

You'll be fine, she had said. You may look like an ordinary Maine Coon, but you have many unique genes that others don't. And believe me, they'll come in handy where you're going, she said. She gave me a big long hug, then she closed the capsule door.

Another feline figure appeared at the window, peering in at me from outside.

"This one looks like an ancient purebred. Never seen one of these on Enceladus before."

Where?! My ears twitched.

"Why doesn't it come out?"

And leave my climate-controlled capsule?!

"It's just shy. Give it some time. Let's go back to the rocks."

Rocks? So Enceladus must not be all ice. Enceladus is a moon of Saturn, as I recall. A very, very long way from Earth. I know that much, but not much more.

Truth be told, I'm an indoor cat. I mean, I can't breathe outside. Besides, it looks pretty cold out there. Cass used to take me out in a bubble on the H-bike, the only way for anyone to breathe inside Earth's atmosphere. Obsolete e-bikes are just burning batteries, Cass would say, and old-fashioned hydrogen bikes are just as slow. Hypersonic H-bikes, on the other hand, she would say, are just the right speed for atmospheric travel.

Indeed, I thought, I could sure use one here and now on Enceladus.

Then I thought again about what Cass had said about my uniquely useful genes, how they might just come in handy someday soon. Cass was a bioengineer. I had no idea what she was talking about, but I trusted she did. At this point, what did I have to lose?

I opened the capsule door.

A rush of cold air enveloped me, propelling me outward and onto the ice. I shivered and coughed furiously, feeling like I was going to explode. But then, I didn't. As I felt my body warming from the inside, my throat calmed and my breathing became effortless. The icy floor felt soft and slushy, cushioning my pads from scintillating shards underfoot.

Magic genes must be kicking in, I thought. Still, I would feel more comfortable on solid rocky ground. Which was nowhere in sight. I started to walk, run, but my paws slipped and slid clumsily on the frictionless ice.

"Silly cat. Don't crawl. Fly."

I looked up to see a svelte feline with bat-like ears, a leopard-like coat and a raccoon-like tail dancing in the air above me. If I wasn't hallucinating, where did she come from?

"Good idea," I said. "Is there an H-bike somewhere around here that I can borrow?"

The serval-like creature flashed a knowing grin.

"Bicycles are for Humans on Earth. We don't need bicycles here, because we can fly."

"We can?"

"Don't fight gravity, let it carry you where you want to go. Use your feathery tail to change directions as you waltz with the winds. Jump. Dance. Fly. On Enceladus, we don't need wings or vehicles to soar high and go far."

So I jumped. I flicked my tail and stretched my legs and, sure enough, found myself soaring above the icy plains. I whipped my tail around and felt the air currents tickling my fur from below and above as I twisted into their pockets. Before I knew it, I was dancing, diving, flying. Not ready to come down again anytime soon.

"So where are the rocks?" I finally asked the spotted dancer, wind rippling through my fur.

"On the other side of Enceladus," she replied with a satisfied smile. "Cross the twilight zone, which divides the northern day from the southern night. Saturn never sets, so it's always in the same place. If you're hungry, go all the way to the South Pole. The Tiger Stripes are where the party is."

Upon which, she took off into the jade ether. Now that she mentioned it, I was famished.

Looking down from above, the planet appeared much smaller, the concave horizon beckoning me forward across a landscape grooved with deep fractures and wide craters. I learned to navigate with my tail, recognizing the Saturnian twilight zone as icy white turned to charcoal gray, while the viscous atmosphere enveloped me in a salty mist.

By the time I arrived at the South Pole it was quite dark, much easier on the eyes. But where were the Tiger Stripes?

"Mind the tiger plume," something snarled.

The what?

I leapt aside as a bellowing geyser of thick cold vapor spewed out from the ice. It smelled of methane, carbon gases, salt and other elements that I couldn't identify.

From the plume emerged the massive, muscular body of a saber-toothed feline carrying a mouthful of jellyfish, which she promptly proceeded to sort and lick on the rocky ice bank. Then she noticed me eyeing her catch.

"What are you, three-fifths hyena? This is my dinner, not yours."

If you can't steal, beg, I thought. I stared at her pathetically with big wet eyes, genetically evolved to melt a human heart.

"Meow..."

Unfortunately, the smilodon was anything but human.

"Scram!" she roared.

I scrammed.

A few heartbeats later, I came across another giant eruption from the ice. This time, the plume carried a whole wave of fishing felines.

Stomach grumbling, I tentatively approached an otter-like cat who appeared to have caught an entire seafood banquet.

"Spare a little jelly?"

She tossed me a polyp.

"That's just an appetizer," she ensued. "There's a whole world down there, you know. Jellyfish aplenty, fat sea slugs and exquisite urchin if you can get around the spines. If you're really lucky, maybe you'll even find a sweet pink axolotl, the ultimate delicacy." The jaguarundi paused long enough to gulp down the rest of her meal. "Just beware the cuttlefish. They master the art of camouflage, can mimic any other creature in the sea and, I'm almost embarrassed to say, have outwitted me and other cats on many occasions with a contemptuous squirt of poison ink. Those cephalopods have mapped out the entire seascape, they know exactly where to hide and how to hunt. So let them have the ocean. After all, we still rule on land."

I looked around at the stark landscape.

"Let's face it, we cats are an invasive species," she continued. "But we're the only creatures on the rocky ice. Everything else lives in the subenceladan sea."

I slurped up the polyp, savoring the subtle tastes and textures of its smooth, malleable mass gliding down my throat. I couldn't help licking the last bits of salt from my whiskers.

The fishing feline was unimpressed.

"So what are you waiting for, a free lunch?"

I blinked. "I can't swim."

"That's too bad, because all the food is under the ice."

On that note, she dove back in.

I sat there alone for a while, watching the other felines feast on their catches. While they were all larger, sleeker and more muscular than I was, each one had a distinct physique, and each seemed to specialize in her own choice of prey. No one was fighting over dessert, I noticed, so there must be plenty to go around.

Once again I reconsidered what Cass had said, about me not being just an ordinary pet cat. Now that I was consumed with hunger, it was high time to set that beast free. I closed my drooling mouth, opened my nostrils to the submarine world of swirling scents, took a deep breath, and dove into the dark sea.

It was surprisingly light beneath the frozen ceiling, and the water became warmer as I descended. As it turned out, swimming was even easier than flying. Suddenly, I was dumbstruck: purple urchins, spotted eels, iridescent jellies, an entire spectrum of nudibranchs in all shapes and colors. So this is what all the fuss is about, I mused, buoyed by the changes in viscosity with the moving tide. I lingered in the depths to savor more sumptuous treats.

By the time I rode the plume back up onto the surface, I was brandishing a plump axolotl as my proud pink-and-white trophy.

My victory was not lost on a tufted lynx-like feline who had apparently been observing me for some time.

"Not bad for a princess house cat."

Excuse me? "I happen to be a Maine Coon tomcat."

She laughed. "We'll see for how long. Momma's boys tend to wither away into the ice. Stronger toms seem to mutate into tabbies as they feel more comfortable in the Stripes. Whatever that means for the future of our species. All I can say is that any time one of us gets injured, our bodies heal almost before we can feel the pain. And besides the long-gone toms, no cat has ever fallen ill. Not sure how we ended up on Enceladus, but we like it here."

She winked. I smiled.

As she slinked away into the mist, I wondered: What if that's what Cass had been up to all that time in the lab? She specialized in engineering the offspring of stray cats, cutting and pasting ancient genes from extinct felines and the prehistoric past—jaguars, snow leopards, saber-toothed tigers... I imagine those neo-felines would have been pretty hard to contain, so the scientists must have sent all the experimental hybrid specimens to Enceladus. If humans couldn't adapt fast enough to survive on any one of Saturn's moons, they must have thought, maybe these pumped-up cats could.

Evidently, some of them did. As did I.

A sharp glint poking out of a narrow fissure caught my eye. Curious, I ventured over for a closer look. What appeared to be an oval piece of glass turned out to be a small mirror attached to a twisted metal bar that led to a dented white tank between two fat gray tires, each stamped with a deformed letter "C". I immediately recognized the remnants of an all-too-familiar H-bike.

Stepping back, I wondered how long I had been asleep in the capsule before I landed on Enceladus. I wondered if humans had since gone extinct, or if there was any multicellular life left on Earth. Maybe all that's left there now are microbes that breathe, eat and excrete rocks, I thought. Inorganic matter like sulfur and nitrate. Static and silent, they'll stay buried deep under the crust, far beneath the ocean mud, sleeping and dreaming for trillions of Earth years. Maybe someday they'll wake up, get a buzz, emerge and evolve into mesoscopic creatures that we can see, relate to, even possibly communicate with. Maybe. Then again, maybe not.

Here, I'm in my element. Enceladus is now home. The Tiger Stripes are for the cats.

Thanks, Cass.

SOPHIE

Summer Jewel Keown

Emily carefully maneuvered her bike down the two thick steps of her new rental house's porch and set it on the cement sidewalk, using one foot to push the kickstand down. As she adjusted the basket mounted between her handlebars, she felt the familiar softness of warm fur rubbing against her bare ankle.

"Hey Soph," she said, bending to scratch the gray cat's ear. "Can you believe it's that time already?"

She straightened up and gazed at the blue sky above her, taking a long breath. The warm air filled her lungs as she closed her eyes. If she could have controlled the weather, this is exactly what she'd pick for a day like this. It just barely kept the ball of anxiety hiding under her rib cage in check. *It will be fine,* she told herself. *One foot in front of the other.*

The cat let out a sound somewhere between a meow and a growl and stood at Emily's feet, staring up.

"Are you sure you want to go?" Emily asked, as though she would get an answer. "I don't know if that's a good idea." The cat peered up at her expectantly. Emily bit her lip, considering. She really shouldn't. But she looked at the cat, she met those green eyes. As though she could resist.

She sighed, conceding. "Oh, all right. The university isn't going to be thrilled, you know. But they can't exactly say no. Just don't blame me when you don't have any fun."

Adjusting her messenger bag and tightening its straps against her, Emily lifted one leg over the bike's steel frame and stood astride.

"Hey ho, let's go," she called, patting her thigh. The cat hopped up on her bent leg, then leapt into the basket. Emily reached to clip the leash attached to the basket to her collar. The cat pulled away, meowing in protest.

"Yes, yes," Emily replied. "I know. But how would it look if I didn't take care of my cat's safety?"

The cat seemed to consider, then settled haughtily into the basket, giving no further protest as Emily clipped her in.

If she was going to do this, Emily decided, she would need proper caffeination. After all, she'd been away for the past two years, and not by her own choice. She began pedaling in the direction of the coffee shop just outside of campus, Sophie keeping a watchful eye from her perch.

She should have realized with the sun out for the first time in a week that there'd be a crowd at the Coffee Corner. As she pulled the bike up and leaned it against a parking meter, she could feel eyes all staring at her. Well, not at her. At her furry companion in the basket. Emily supposed she couldn't blame them.

"Excuse me," a girl said from behind her, as Emily looped the cord of her lock around the meter. "How did you train your cat to ride like that?"

Emily turned and smiled. A tall girl, probably in her early twenties, with long black braids flipped over her shoulders, stood grinning at Sophie. Of course. Who could resist a chill cat on a bicycle?

"Oh, I'm just lucky," Emily replied. "She likes traveling."

"She really doesn't try to run away?"

"What, and have to find her own food? No way."

At that the cat turned and gave Emily a withering look, as though she understood what was being said and thoroughly disapproved.

"I'm only kidding, Sophie," Emily apologized. "I know you could be the best mouser out there if you wanted to."

"Oh, that's hilarious," the girl said. "Can I pet her?"

"I'll do you one better. If I run in and grab a coffee, would you mind watching her for a minute?" Emily knew Sophie didn't really need watching, but she wouldn't begrudge her a little attention.

The girl's smile widened. "Happy to!"

"Perfect. I'll be right back. Just leave her collar clipped in, if you don't mind. She loves getting scratched behind her ears, if you want to make friends for life. Oh, shoot, and I'm Emily, by the way."

"Genevieve."

"Pretty name."

"Thanks." The girl turned her attention to Sophie, cooing and petting her lightly. The cat pushed her head against the girl's fingers, leaning in. *So much for loyalty*, Emily thought wryly.

The line inside was long, but moving quickly. She checked her watch. Hopefully her dirty chai wouldn't make her late for class. She was already dreading it enough already without the additional attention she'd surely get from strolling in after the lecture began. Especially with her somewhat unconventional companion.

She managed to get her drink quickly enough, and headed back out to her bike, where Sophie's new friend Genevieve had clearly fallen in love with her already. She did have that effect on people. Emily should know.

"Thanks so much," Emily said. "Looks like you have a new friend there."

"She's so sweet," Genevieve gushed. "And so pretty too. She just has the softest fur. What an angel."

"Oh don't worry. She's still a cat. She bites my ankles in the morning if I don't feed her quickly enough."

Genevieve laughed. "Worth it though, I'm sure."

"Definitely."

There was an awkward pause. Emily stooped down and unlocked the bike.

"Well, thanks," she said to the girl. "Guess I'd better be off."

The girl shuffled her feet and looked nervous. "Would you, maybe, want to hang out sometime?"

Emily smiled nervously. "Are you asking for me, or for Sophie?"

"Either. Both. I mean. God, I'm so bad at this." The girl blushed and looked down at the ground.

Emily's stomach dropped. It wasn't that Genevieve wasn't attractive. She was. A few years ago Emily would have been thrilled that someone like her was asking her on a date. But now... Plus, clearly the girl didn't do magic. Even though she had a perfectly witchy-sounding name. Not that she would have been interested if the girl had been a witch. Or would she? Emily tried to clear her thoughts. She definitely wasn't ready for this yet. She didn't know if she ever would be.

Sophie was watching them from the basket, still gleaning every last pet from her new friend's hand. She looked up at Emily expectantly. Emily was tempted to tell her to drop it, but she didn't want to cross that line from cute and quirky into full-blown talking-to-my-cat lady.

What should she do? Exchange numbers and then make excuses to avoid actually getting together? Or just be honest and turn her down now and trade future awkward exchanges for one right now? She'd forgotten how much she sucked at dating. At least now she had a good excuse.

"Sure," Emily said, giving a smile that she hoped promised friendship and not much more. "But I must warn you. I'm just starting classes so my life is going to be a little insane."

"Oh really? Where do you go?"

"Havernell College. Just up the road."

"Oh! I hear that's really hard to get into."

"Well," Emily laughed. "It can't be too hard, since they let me in." *Lies already*, she thought. Even if there weren't other solid reasons, the lies alone would mean she could never go out with this girl. But, they were necessary, she knew that. What would the normals do if they found out the obscure private liberal arts college was so much more than it looked?

They exchanged numbers, then Emily grabbed her bike and began pedaling away, carefully balancing her drink on her handlebar. Sophie meowed and settled back into her basket.

"Don't you even start," she said.

As she biked across the invisible line dividing campus from the rest of the town, Emily felt the barrier identify her, then grant her entry. At least that was working. If it hadn't approved her, she'd have found herself riding off in another direction, with no real memory of where she'd been going or why. It was a much more effective way to protect the school than handing out plastic student IDs.

She was going to be late, there was no way around it. Great. Her first day back and she was already going to start with a mark against her. Maybe the class wouldn't begin on time. Or maybe no one would notice her. Maybe, but unlikely.

Emily parked the bike at a rack near Sampson Hall and locked it up as quickly as she could. Unhooking Sophie's collar from the bike rack, she opened up her messenger bag and held it out. Sophie looked at it skeptically.

"Get in the bag, Sophie," she said. She knew how ridiculous that sounded. She said a lot of ridiculous things these days. Emily sighed. "If you don't get in the bag, I can't take you inside. You know you can't just roam the campus. I'm sorry."

Sophie glared at her, then leapt gracefully into the open bag. Emily adjusted the strap, then hustled inside.

There was no time to admire the stateliness of the building, one of only a few to have survived from when the school was founded in the 1700s. She raced up the steps to the third floor classroom, her lungs protesting the exertion. Sophie made little noises of protest as her bag jostled around, but Emily couldn't reassure her anymore. They'd talked about this.

Pushing the door open, the professor was already writing an equation on the board. He turned toward her at the sound of her entry and Emily gritted her teeth, ready to take a warning. Instead he simply raised one eyebrow and nodded toward an empty seat. Right in the front, of course. So much for being under the radar.

She tried not to make eye contact with her classmates as she passed, ignored the giggles and whispers. After all, she'd expected it.

She carefully hung the strap of the messenger bag over the back of her chair. Maybe Sophie would just take a quiet nap for the duration of class. As though on cue, the cat poked her head out of the flap. Someone gasped behind her, but Emily didn't turn around. She already knew that everyone was staring at her and Sophie.

"Be cool," she whispered to the cat, who of course, immediately leapt out of the bag and lay down in the aisleway between desks. The buzz of chatter behind them amplified until Professor Mason cleared his throat loudly.

"Does anyone want to summarize chapter one for us?" he asked, fixing a stern expression on the class. The room hushed. "In that case I'd advise paying attention."

Emily tried to focus on the lecture, but the words washed over her like water. Calculus probably wasn't the best choice for a morning class, but she needed to catch up on all she'd missed. And magic was nothing without math, she knew that. She hoped she could catch up later by reading the textbook. It wasn't as though any of these people were likely to loan her their notes.

She spent the next hour pretending to be listening intently, while feeling her fifteen or so classmates stare daggers into the back of her head. Finally, class was over. Emily packed up her things slowly until everyone else had finally left the room. When she rose to leave, Prof. Mason was standing over her.

"Welcome back, Miss Salton."

"Oh. Um, thank you," she stammered. She'd always found him a little intimidating.

"Can I give you a little advice?" he asked. She nodded. "You would likely draw less attention if you… left the cat at home. They would move on to other inane gossip."

"Maybe, but it wouldn't be fair."

Mr. Mason sighed and adjusted his glasses. "I suppose not. Well then, we will see you again Wednesday. Read the chapters closely, there may be a quiz." He bent down to Sophie.

"May I?" he asked, and held his hand out to her, palm up. The cat blinked up at him but didn't move away. He ran a finger lightly across her head.

"Sophie was always a favorite of mine," he said. "I was very sad to hear what happened."

"It was an accident," Emily said, staring at the floor. She could feel tears coming to her eyes.

"I know. Trust me, we all know."

Emily knew if she tried to talk about it she would fully cry, and she still had to get through two more classes before going home for the evening. She couldn't show up to her Magical History of the 20th Century class with red eyes if she didn't want people to stare even more, if that was even possible. She quickly thanked Prof. Mason and excused herself, gathering up Sophie back in her bag.

The rest of the day was much the same: quiet whispers and chatter behind her everywhere she went. At least no one had been brave enough to say anything to her face, but surely that couldn't last as they became used to her again. She just had one more stop before she could leave: the Dean's office.

She'd been dreading it, but if she wanted to get her magic reinstated, it was necessary. Standing outside the carved wood door of the office, Emily steeled herself. She hid her bag underneath a nearby bench, whispering to Sophie to wait for her there. For once, the cat didn't protest. She knew how important this was.

One hand aloft, Emily took a deep breath, and knocked.

"Come in," a deep voice answered. She pushed her way inside.

The dean was bent over a stack of papers on her desk, her gray hair speckled with light from the window behind her. She looked up as Emily entered.

"Ah. Miss Salton. I wondered when I would see your face. Please, sit." Emily sat in the ancient armchair across the desk from her

"Dean Delvaux, good afternoon." She tried not to stammer. The Dean's expression was impossible to read.

"As I recall, it's been some time since you were... last on our campus."

"Indeed. And thank you for seeing me."

"You understand why you're in my office?" She adjusted her glasses, peering at her over the rim.

"I do. And I want you to know that I'm very glad to be back."

The Dean looked her over, as though evaluating if she could be trusted to roam the halls again. Emily knew this was just a formality—she wouldn't have been let in at all otherwise—but the Dean still made her feel like she was on trial. Not that there had been a trial, not exactly. A committee, yes. A decision to expel her, yes. And eventually, an appeal that was granted, on a probationary basis.

"You understand the terms, then." The dean shuffled through her drawers and pulled out a folder marked First Year Release. Emily was so embarrassed. The dean offered her the form and a pen and Emily signed it quickly. She didn't need to read it. She already knew what it said, having signed it four years ago when she actually was a First Year. With her signature she promised not to misuse her magic and to practice her exercises only where and when she was prescribed by an instructor, under penalty of revocation. It was a small price to pay to be able to do magic again.

The moment she handed the form back to the dean, that familiar tingle shot up from her fingers into her arms. She closed her eyes as it came into her chest, spreading through all of her veins and muscles. Squeezing her eyelids closed, she willed herself not to cry. She'd missed this so much.

The sun was setting in brilliant shades of blue and pink as she finally rode back up to her house. She unhooked Sophie's collar from the leash in the basket and the cat quickly leapt down and stretched out her limbs, as though she'd had a long day too. And maybe she had.

Emily made a quick dinner, then sat at the kitchen table trying to read her textbook and eat pasta at the same time. After reading the same page three times without retaining a single word or idea, she slammed it closed. Sophie, napping on the chair next to her, startled and scowled up at her.

"Sorry, Soph." She leaned back in her chair. In the old days, she could have vented about her day, shared stories and empathy. Now, there was no one left to listen. Except Sophie. Not that she could talk back. But that gave her a thought... well, but she wasn't supposed to do any magic at home. Not unless she had a specific assignment, the Dean had just said, until she finished out her semester and re-tested out of the basic safety course. How embarrassing, but she supposed she understood. And after two years without her powers, she really shouldn't go misusing them right away.

Still, no one would notice just a little spell. And it was fully night now. All the other witches and magicians would be doing their own things at this hour. *Oh, screw it,* she thought.

She got up and started rustling through the kitchen cabinets, grabbing a bowl and measuring cups, some salt and dried herbs. Frankincense, rue, agrimony. She was almost out of mugwort but she'd use what was left. Walking through the house, she collected half a dozen candles—not the preferred spell-casting kind, more the "I didn't know what to get you for your birthday" kind. Setting the motley collection on the living room floor in a cluster, she looked skeptically at it. Well, it might do.

Scattering the salt in a circle, she measured the herbs carefully into the bowl. Then she placed the candles around the circle. Really she should measure the angles between the bowl and each candle, make sure the circle wasn't lopsided, but she didn't have a tape measure ready. If this worked, she'd have to get one for next time. For now she'd just estimate.

The final touch, Emily rose and fetched the cat brush from the living room table next to the couch. It still had tufts of fur in it from the last time she'd groomed Sophie, and she pulled a bit free. Returning to the circle, she added it to the bowl.

Grabbing a matchbook out of a drawer, she ripped one out and struck its head across the strip, succeeding on her second try. The flame burned brightly in her hand. Kneeling down, she lit the candles one by one, as quickly as she could, the flame licking her fingertips. Then she dropped it into the bowl. The herbs resisted for a moment, then caught fire. A few moments later the fur did as well, filling the room with an acrid odor not quite masked by the nice-smelling herbs. Emily wrinkled her nose. No one ever said magic had a great smell to it.

She rose and flipped off the lights. The candles glowed, casting their light against the bare white wall that she hadn't yet adorned with any photos or posters. She sat, legs crossed in front of the candles, closed her eyes, and waited.

From the kitchen, Emily heard Sophie leap down to the wooden floor. She opened her eyes and looked up as the cat strode into the room, and walked between the candles and the wall. She really was a beautiful cat, Emily thought. But of course she was.

She watched the cat's shadow cast by the candles onto the plain white wall. Then she spoke a few words, snatches of Old English and Latin, quietly yet clearly. She waited. It took some time, and she thought maybe it wouldn't work. Maybe she just couldn't work magic well anymore. Maybe she'd lost her ability during the ban of the past two years. Maybe she'd lost her confidence.

The shadow started to flicker, stretch, change. Emily straightened up, letting the magic work, her blood humming. The shadow grew into the shape of a young woman, her arms stretching out, fingers splaying and contracting. Her head moved slowly from side to side. Emily would recognize that profile anywhere, its strong nose, her long hair flowing down behind her. She could imagine the ever-present smile.

"Oh, Sophie," she whispered. "There you are"

The shadow nodded yes. Emily felt tears drip down her face, but she just let them run. She needed to concentrate to keep the spell stable. She could feel it wavering, her magic a little rusty from disuse, her materials clearly inferior.

"It is still you in there. Thank goodness. I mean, I know that, I can feel it. Even though they warned me that you might lose yourself, I know you're you.

"I miss you so much. I know you're right here with me, and I'm glad for it. But I miss talking with you, laughing with you, hell, even fighting with you.

"Two years now. They said it might wear off. I've been hoping every day that I'd wake up and you'd be sprawled out next to me on the bed, arms and feet instead of paws. Right where you used to be. But instead you're still pooping in a box." Sophie meowed. "Yes, I know it's just as sanitary as a toilet. I'm just saying."

Her phone chimed from the kitchen. The shadow cocked her head toward the sound.

"Oh who cares about that?" Emily asked. Like anyone ever texted her anymore anyway. It dawned on her that it might be that girl from earlier. Shadow Sophie must have had the same thought. She pointed a shadow finger toward the sound, made her shadow hand into a phone and mimed holding it up to her head.

"You're hilarious," Emily said. "Like I have any interest in that girl. In any girls who aren't you." The shadow shook her head.

"I don't care," Emily continued. "I don't want to move on. I don't want someone else, I want you back. I mean, you're here, even if you don't look like you. And hell, if I never can change you back, it wouldn't be fair to you for me to go out with someone else. It's not like you can. Not that I didn't notice you loving getting your ear scratched earlier." She couldn't help but tease. Without a little humor, she would have lost her mind by now.

Shadow Sophie made a heart with her hands, then mimed blowing a kiss.

Emily was fully sobbing now. The shadow flickered. The magic was breaking down and in a moment it would be gone.

"I love you, Soph," she whispered. Tears blurred her eyes. Wiping them away, she looked up, and the shadow was gone.

Cat Sophie strode up to her and leapt into her lap. Emily looked down at her, into her cat eyes, black pupils surrounded by a green that matched Sophie's from before. She could see her in there, still, even if everyone else saw her as a cat. Just her unconventional familiar, a rumor of a spell gone wrong. She bent down toward the cat, and Sophie rubbed her face against Emily's.

The phone chimed again, reminding her of the message waiting. She didn't care. She was going to get all of her magic back, study all she could, and someday, even if it were years away, she was going to bring Sophie back. And until then, they still had each other.

THE NINTH CYCLE

Gretchin Lair

I t was the first perfect spring day of the year. A sunbeam slanted just so onto a grey tabby cat resting on a wicker chair, her eyes peacefully closed, her ears occasionally twitching as a breeze ruffled through. The rest of the porch remained shaded, and two dogs lay nearby: an all-black German Shepherd with fine white hairs around his muzzle, and a young border collie with a black patch over half of his face. Past the screen door, they could all hear sounds of brunch being cleared, but it was such a beautiful day neither of the dogs longed to be inside begging for scraps. People strolled about the neighborhood, admiring the green leafing trees or crocuses rising from winter's earth.

Suddenly Shadow, the older dog, lifted his head, ears perked. Before the bicycle could even be seen, he lunged for the fence, barking. Whidbey leaped down the steps to follow him in a flash, also barking. Sage stayed in her chair, keeping her eyes closed as she heard the bicyclist curse, the frame squeaking and wheels ticking as it picked up speed.

After the bicycle passed, the dogs returned to the porch. Shadow collapsed, panting, while Whidbey sniffed up the stairs and around the chair.

"Did you see that?" Whidbey asked Sage, tail wagging. "Wasn't that fun?"

Sage opened one green eye, then the other. She yawned languorously, her mouth suddenly wide with teeth.

"Why do you chase bikes, pup?" she asked. Whidbey was no longer the cute puppy he had been a year ago, but Sage was an old cat. Whidbey would always be a pup to her.

Whidbey sat down. "I don't know! It's fun! Shadow likes it!"

After a pause, Shadow said, "They run fast."

Sage said, "But they pose no threat. Do you chase the clouds? They pass in the same way."

Whidbey cocked his head to the side, one floppy ear bending. "That's a good point."

Shadow huffed. "Bikes! I hate them. They have no respect. Did you hear? This one cursed us while we defended our territory."

Sage said, "Faults in others may actually be reflections of our own afflictions. What you resist will persist."

Whidbey looked both confused and thoughtful at the same time. Shadow huffed again, his lips flapping as he settled his nose between his paws. "Cats! You will never understand."

They lapsed into a congenial silence, enjoying the fresh scents of a new season. Sage closed her eyes again. Whidbey paced the porch, interested in a pile of leaves that had never been swept from the fall, before settling next to Shadow. The neighbor's wind chimes rang gently in melodic meditation.

Suddenly Shadow stiffened, then raced for the fence. Whidbey followed, barking in arrhythmic harmony. Two young men riding bicycles passed, one almost swerving into the other with surprise. "Stupid dogs!" he yelled. Shadow, offended, began barking harder, pawing at the gate. "I'm not stupid! You're stupid! Get off that thing and fight me like a dog, you mutts! If I catch you I'll bite bite bite!"

"Geez, Shadow!" Whidbey said. "I thought this was supposed to be fun!"

Shadow ignored him and kept barking, though the bicycles were long gone.

"Shadow! Shut up!" yelled two women from the house in unison.

Whidbey, bored, wandered back to the porch, stopping to investigate an old mole hill on the lawn first. He lay near the chair, looking up at Sage with one brown eye and one blue eye.

Sage's sharp feline features softened. "What troubles you, pup?"

Whidbey whined softly. "I thought it was fun to chase things! But I don't think it's fun for Shadow. Why is he like that?"

Sage sat up with such a fluid motion Whidbey couldn't tell she was ever lying down at all. She began washing a paw. "He is at the mercy of old habits. Shadow may not even know why he does it anymore."

"Why don't you chase things?" Whidbey asked.

Sage chuckled, a soft sound like a cross between a purr and a sigh. "Oh, I used to, pup. Ask any crow in the neighborhood. But I am almost at the end of my eighth cycle, and I no longer confuse duty and desire."

Whidbey tilted his head. "Your eighth cycle?"

Sage stretched. "All cats are reborn up to nine times, at which point we reach enlightenment. Over and over again we encounter what we need to learn most. With each cycle we rise wiser than before."

Whidbey's eyes were wide, his mouth open slightly. "Reborn? What does that feel like?"

Sage said softly, her eyes distant: "It is like the moon on water. It is like seeing beyond the dark."

Whidbey clearly didn't think this was a satisfying answer, but he knew better than to say so. Instead he asked, "What about dogs? Do we have cycles? Do we ever reach enlightenment?"

Sage began washing behind her ear. She said, "Perhaps. I am not a dog, so I do not know. But I do know that all beings can aspire to the patience, detachment, and flexibility of cats."

She glanced at Shadow, who was still at the gate, barking intermittently. "But Shadow is a dog, so he has a harder time because of his nature. You, too, pup. You will need to practice mindfulness to enjoy the comings and goings of the world without being triggered by them. If you are mindful, things will become as clear as a bowl of fresh water."

Whidbey scratched behind an ear, trying to understand. His dog tags jangled.

After a final bark, Shadow returned to the porch. "Curs," he growled. His tongue lolled from his mouth, exhausted from the exertion.

Sage said mildly, "Do not find fault with others. If they behave wrongly, there is no need to make yourself suffer."

Shadow said stiffly, "I'm not suffering!"

"Then why are you so mad?" Whidbey asked.

Shadow burst out, "Nobody appreciates everything I do to keep us safe! There are only two of us. We have to bark like we're a bigger pack! Blitz taught me that!" Shadow had been a shelter dog, and he often told stories of the other dog he had lived with in his first family.

Sage settled back onto her cushion. "I only meow when it improves the silence."

Shadow said, "Well, that's great if you're a cat. But I'm a dog! I won't apologize for it. I'm still a wolf inside."

An awkward silence. Sage lifted one leg and began washing it, while Whidbey flopped on his side, chewing an old ball near the chair. Shadow relaxed, lowering himself onto the porch, his nose hanging over the top step. A hummingbird hovered nearby, chirping and dipping into the bleeding heart before zipping off to another yard. The sun had shifted to cover the whole chair, so Sage stretched out, her eyes dazzling in the light.

Shadow suddenly looked up. He ran down the porch steps, barking and pushing against the gate to stand on his hind legs. Whidbey followed after him, less enthusiastically than usual.

A middle-aged woman on a white step-through bicycle pedaled by slowly, clearly enjoying the day until Shadow started barking. She startled, losing control of her bike. It slipped and she fell into the street, crying out.

Just then, the gate gave way. Shadow was out in an instant and running towards the woman. She glanced up, terrified, and scrambled to put the bike between her and Shadow. "No!" she shouted. "No! Go away! Go home!"

Whidbey, who had never been outside the gate without a leash, was exhilarated. He ran towards them, too, barking happily. Shadow stopped about two feet away from the woman, barking, but Whidbey leaped around her, paws flailing, mouth open. The woman saw his teeth and shrieked, kicking at him. "No! Bad dog! No!" Whidbey yelped, clearly not understanding why the woman was so angry at him.

The screen door banged open. "Shadow! No! Shadow! Stop!" Two women in lazy Sunday clothes ran towards the dogs. One with short curly hair grabbed Shadow by his collar, hauling him back. The other, a woman with a long ponytail, stood behind until she realized Whidbey was still barking and ran towards him. Whidbey took a couple of steps back, avoiding her grasp.

"Whidbey! No!" She reached towards him and he danced back with a high-pitched bark. Her ponytail whipped around as she tried to catch him. He turned and started running down the street. "Whidbey! Come, Whidbey! Come!" He stopped, turning towards her, but as she ran towards him he ran off again. "Whidbey!" He slowed, turned. The woman from the house was now sitting on her heels on the sidewalk, patting the ground next to her and smiling. "Come on, Whidbey! Come on! Good boy!"

He approached cautiously, and when he was close enough to her, she grabbed him by his collar and scooped him into her arms. "Bad dog, Whidbey," she said, not unkindly. "Baaaaad dog."

The women escorted Shadow and Whidbey back to the yard. The short-haired woman checked the gate twice to make sure it was secure, then they both continued apologizing to the woman with the bike, who was examining a scrape on her knee.

Whidbey ran straight to the porch without sniffing anything and hid behind the chair. Shadow stormed up the steps.

"What's the matter with you, pup?" Shadow snapped.

Whidbey whined, groveling. "I'm a bad dog! I'm sorry!"

Shadow pressed his alpha advantage. "This is serious! You never, ever bite! You just bark!"

Whidbey said, "But I didn't! I didn't bite! And you said —!"

"Forget what I said! If you bite, they could take you away! Blitz got taken away! I won't lose you, too!"

Sage leaped lightly from the chair to sit beside Whidbey. Facing Shadow, she said, "You contributed to this. Your words and your actions were not in alignment. See, now, how the cycle turns. The young dog suffers for the anger of the old."

The women returned to the house. The one with the long ponytail bent over and stroked Sage as she passed. "Teach these dogs a thing or two about chilling out, okay, Sage?" Sage bent her head against the woman's hand, indulging her attention.

After the women were inside, Sage turned to Whidbey. "You're only doing what others do, pup, as Shadow learned to do. Do not concern yourself with outside judgments: good cat, bad cat, it is all the same. These names pass like the spring breeze and are gone." She jumped back onto her chair, even though the sunlight had moved on.

Shadow looked as if he was going to object when his ears flicked and he tensed. He had clearly heard another bicycle and was trying to restrain himself. Whidbey watched him closely. A man with a jaunty cap riding a cargo bike passed, carrying potting soil and a flat of garden annuals. Shadow practically vibrated with concentration, until finally he couldn't contain himself anymore and leaped off the porch. His bark was half-hearted, though, and he stayed about a foot from the fence. The bike was quickly out of view.

"Shadow!" shouted the women simultaneously from inside the house.

Whidbey moved to the head of the stairs, watching Shadow. "You said you've had eight cycles, but I've only got one. How am I going to get it right?"

Sage smiled, though Whidbey could only tell from a slight twitch of her whiskers. "You don't need me to tell you right from wrong, pup. That's a start. I am tasked to help others reach enlightenment before my ninth cycle, and you can help even with just one. Who will teach Shadow if we do not?"

As if summoned, Shadow trotted back to the porch. "Well, I guess I can let him off with a warning this time."

Whidbey's tail wagged once. "That was quick. I think you're learning, Shadow!"

Shadow narrowed his eyes as he sat. "Learning? What do you have to teach me, pup?"

"Sometimes it's fun just to watch the bikes go by," Whidbey said, his natural smile widening. "They seem really happy. Don't you want to be happy, Shadow?"

"I see the cat has her claws into you," Shadow said, resignedly.

"Release your attachment to the world as you wish it to be and you can be happy with the world as it is," Sage said, closing her eyes serenely. "I am a cat, but I want for nothing and answer to no one. I no longer need the string or the cardboard box. I —"

Sage stopped suddenly. Her eyes snapped open, pupils dilating. So quickly the dogs almost didn't register it, she leaped from the chair and slipped past the screen door. They heard a woman stumble and cry out: "Damnit, Sage!" The dogs scrambled to the screen to peer inside, where they could see Sage rubbing against the woman's legs as she opened a can of cat food.

Shadow grinned at Whidbey. "I guess nobody's perfect."

"Not in this cycle, anyway," Whidbey said.

THE CERTAINTY OF DANGER

Monique Cuillerier

In the dream, I am looking through a shimmering force field that stretches in all directions.

On the other side is the lab where I used to work. I can identify it with certainty even though it is crowded and noisy in a way the lab never was.

My eyes pick out Cady and Aliosha amongst the crowd. They are working at the powder diffractometer along the far wall and I raise my hand to get their attention.

But before they can notice me, there is a sudden, loud noise and a flash of white that obscures the entire room.

There is something I ought to do, but I can't remember what it is.

Then everything is red and it begins to clear.

Where Cady and Aliosha were standing, there is now a gaping hole.

. . .

In my mind there was a message.

Warning. A decompression event has progressed to level two. Prepare for imminent evacuation. Warning. A decompression event...

That was all I needed to come completely awake. Even after all these years with the neural implant, the sensation of connection with the network is a peculiar one. It is a thought but not a thought.

The sleeping area was dark, but there was a flashing red light in the other room. I was wide awake, but it still took me a moment to remember that, while I was still on Mars, I was at the outpost, alone.

Pulling on my base layers, I made my way to the control panel in the common room, pushing aside the lingering memory of the familiar dream. I stepped into the pants of my surface suit and pulled them up. They fit snugly to provide the counter-pressure necessary to keep me alive outside of the outpost.

My heart began to pound and I breathed in.

Slowly.

I looked at the panel, but before I could locate a reason for the alarm, the message returned with greater urgency.

Evacuate now. Evacuate now. Interior atmosphere will be unsustainable in one point five minutes. Evacuate...

Breathe out.

I grabbed my helmet and headed towards the airlock, closing the interior door behind me. Sticking the helmet on my head, I sealed it against my suit and started the process to equalize the airlock's pressure with the surface.

The airlock served as a garage and storage area as well. I gave my bike a quick once over to make sure the Emergency Surface Tent and food supply pack were there. Then I got on the bike and waited.

I took a deep breath as the exterior door began to dial open.

None of this should be happening, not here.

I exhaled slowly. I needed to pay attention.

So far, so good.

And then I cycled out onto the dusty red surface.

•   •   •

I slowly rode around the building's exterior, trying to locate the point of decompression. Unfortunately, it was easy to find.

A tear in the fabric of the exterior layer gaped open like a mouth. Clearly it had gone through to the interior wall in order to trigger the decompression alarm.

And that was when panic pushed through my focus. I could barely catch my breath. I put my right foot down in the red dust to steady myself, the bike still between my legs.

In. I felt the air entering at my nostrils.

I looked at the tear again and then had to look away. Had the tear been smaller, I could have tried to fix it. But as it was, it required more technical expertise than I possessed.

Out. My lungs emptied.

Briefly, I allowed myself to wonder what had caused the decompression, but it didn't matter. I needed to figure out what to do next.

The first step was to contact the regional base on Lunae Planum.

"This is Teena Cardinal, at Outpost Carl Sagan," I began hesitantly, but there was no response.

I repeated myself, but to no avail.

Without giving myself time to reflect, or begin to worry, I changed the setting.

"This is Outpost Sagan, Specialist Teena Cardinal speaking," I said again, but this time I was happily interrupted.

"This is the Northern Hemispheric Facility. We read you, Outpost Sagan."

The relief of knowing someone else would tell me what to do rushed through me.

"Northern, the outpost has experienced a decompression incident."

"Acknowledged. There was a strong marsquake with an epicentre west of your location."

"I attempted to contact Lunae base without response."

"There has been no contact with Lunae," Northern responded briskly and then continued. "Are you injured? Is your bike damaged?"

"The bike is fine and I'm okay."

"Can you fix the damage to the outpost?"

"No." A lump of failure lurked in a corner of my mind.

"Can you head to...," there was a pause. "... Outpost Mutch?"

"Can you repeat, Northern?"

"Can you head to Outpost Mutch? You'll be heading towards us and you can check on Specialist Lorrin. There has been no report from them." They paused again. "Not that it means anything. We hadn't had a report from you until now."

I tried to smile, but my stomach twisted. "Have many of the outposts not reported in?"

"Yes, but it hasn't been very long. Despite the strength of the quake, we don't have reports of serious damage."

That felt comforting, until it occurred to me that if there was serious damage—or injury or death—they wouldn't be able to report in.

I took another deep breath and let it out.

"We have begun to deploy first responders," Northern continued. "It would be helpful if you went to Mutch. We'll send a team in that direction to pick all of you up."

I was not entirely comfortable with the suggested plan, but was happy to follow instructions.

•   •   •

There was supposed to be a path.

I had never cycled all the way from Sagan to Mutch before, but there was a three metre wide strip that was usually cleared to make it easier. Now it was littered with all manner of rocks and loose debris.

As I made my way forward, a part of my mind wandered. I had pursued this job at the outpost, very specifically, wanting nothing more than to be responsible for no one but myself.

The reason for this was not complicated, as my recurring dream attested. I had previously worked in the main UNSpace research facility, adjacent to, but separate from, Curie City. I was doing research on biosignatures. Until the accident.

It wasn't the first such tragedy and it wouldn't be the last. Living on Mars would never be completely safe. But two people died and they were two people I knew. I had worked with Cady and Aliosha for three years. I saw them every day.

But when the outer wall of the facility was breached as a result of a sudden, catastrophic fire, Cady and Aliosha were on the wrong side of the containment door as it descended and sealed itself.

They were not far away and I saw their faces clearly as they realized what was happening. But they could not get back quickly enough and my attempts to override the door failed.

After the accident, I was put on medical leave, as was everyone else who had been involved, and before it was over, I had applied for a transfer.

And I was happy in my little outpost, by myself, with no one depending on me, no one to worry about. No one who would suffer as a result of my ineptitude except myself.

I spent my days extracting deep core samples and measuring geological activity. It wasn't exciting, but I wasn't looking for exciting.

The thing I had not fully appreciated, when I took the job, was just how far apart everything was. Intellectually, I knew, but the practical implications were something else.

It was a long trek from my outpost to the next. Typically, I was picked up and dropped off by a mass transporter that made the rounds of the research outposts with supplies and staff. I used the bike to reach sampling sites.

There is a simple elegance to Mars that I have grown to love in my time here. The wide, reaching plains and spectacular mountains, the valleys of all sizes, a landscape almost entirely unbroken by signs of human interference until you find an outpost or a lander or a rover. The lack of plant material only adds to the stark beauty.

I kept going until I was too tired to continue. There was no point in overextending myself, as I knew I could not reach Mutch without resting.

"Northern? This is Specialist Cardinal."

"We read you, Specialist."

"I am stopping to rest. Have you heard from Outpost Mutch?"

"Not yet."

That was that, and I turned my attention to the emergency tent. When connected to the environmental controls on the bike, it would provide me with a living environment while I had a full cycle of sleep and a meal.

I cleared a space for the tent on the ground, moving the larger rocks out of the way, then I spread out a ground sheet. Working in the surface suit was always awkward, but the tent went up quickly.

Finally, I crawled in through the small airlock and went to sleep, pushing aside the lurking fear.

•   •   •

No damage was visible as I approached Outpost Mutch.

I circled around it, but only detected a slight shifting of the foundation.

I approached the airlock and sent the command to open it, remaining on my bike as I did so.

"Outpost Mutch? This is Specialist Cardinal from Outpost Sagan. I'm here to check on you."

I expected no response and received none. The outer airlock door opened and I pedalled in.

Once inside the outpost, three things were immediately clear:

There was indeed no damage and the environment inside the outpost was safe.

Specialist Lorrin was nowhere to be found and their bike was gone.

There was a cat sitting on a sofa in the common room.

Who are you? the cat improbably said.

Not out loud, which was the only thing that would have been more surprising, but directly into my mind.

I've had a neural link implant for years now, but I've only ever used it to connect with a computer. I had heard about their use in animals, but never come across it myself.

I'm Specialist Teena Cardinal. I work at Outpost Sagan. What's your name? I walked over and sat down on the chair facing the sofa.

Bastet, the small black cat said. It seemed an aspirational name for such a cute and tiny animal.

Where is Specialist Lorrin?

They went out to work.

When? I asked.

Bastet looked at me steadily, as if it were a ridiculous question to ask a cat. Which it probably was. The entire exchange was surreal, though.

Then they said, *A while ago. I slept and ate and slept more and now you are here.* I considered that and decided to call Northern back. This was far outside of my comfort level.

"Northern? This is Specialist Cardinal."

"This is Northern. Where are you, Specialist?"

"I'm at Mutch. Specialist Lorrin is not here. But there is a cat."

There was a pause. "Yes, Bastet."

"So I gathered."

There was another pause.

"Does, uh, Bastet know where Lorrin went?"

I could not believe I was having this conversation. "They said Lorrin went out to work. I'm not sure we have a, um, common way of thinking about time."

"You need to go and find Lorrin."

I considered that. My initial thought was to ask why or just say no.

"Of course," I said instead.

"We'll send you the possible coordinates," they offered. "Take Bastet with you. I'm sure they'll be of help. They are very clever, good problem solvers."

I looked at the cat skeptically, but agreed to Northern's request.

I'm coming with you, Bastet said as I began to gather supplies together.

I guess, I answered, still not happy about it.

I have a carrier in the airlock, they continued, as they followed me around. *You wear it on your back. It attaches to the environmental console on the bike.*

I stopped and looked steadily at the little fluffy black cat now sitting at my feet. It was disconcerting to have a conversation with such a creature. My instinct was to pick them up or maybe scratch their neck, not to have a conversation with them.

Okay, I finally said, although taking care of a cat while looking for a lost scientist seemed ridiculous.

·   ·   ·

Come on, I called to Bastet as I opened the carrier. It was a rounded oval and easily slipped over my shoulders and around my waist like a pack intended for hiking. The bottom part of the carrier would provide for both of our oxygen needs.

I returned my focus to Bastet, who was now waiting in the carrier, ready for me to seal it. I gave them a quick, embarrassed scratch on the side of their neck, which they leaned into, before I closed it.

Once everything was stowed in the trailer on my bike, I got on and leaned back slightly so Bastet's carrier could connect to the bike's onboard environmental controls.

You good? I asked the cat.

Air is coming through, I'm ready, they answered.

I remained unsettled, but began the process to open the airlock.

We rode out on the surface. The directions that Northern sent me were displayed on the inside of my visor and I kept an eye on it as we went.

The previously soothing landscape now left me feeling anxious. I did not feel prepared for this task.

Everything was so far apart. And I wasn't a rescue specialist.

I just wanted to find Lorrin and bring them back to the outpost so that the truck from Northern could retrieve us.

And me, chimed in Bastet.

I had been thinking too clearly, I thought ruefully. It was unlike communicating with an AI or robot, who could be asked to turn off or ignore your thoughts.

But there was a sense of comfort in having Bastet with me on this journey. It was not a feeling I was entirely familiar with, but I did not completely dislike it.

· · ·

The location, when we got there, was a sample site much like many that I had worked on. It was only distinguished by bright blue tape tied to 3D printed plastic posts delineating specific sample areas.

First, I cycled around the area to see if there was anything unusual, but nothing stood out. Certainly core samples had been extracted in the marked areas, but that was all.

Do you see anything? I asked Bastet, feeling silly.

Lorrin always uses blue tape, they offered.

I got off the bike and looked around more carefully, but there was nothing else.

"Northern Hemisphere, this is Specialist Cardinal. Do you read me?" I called eventually, not wanting to miss anything before reporting in.

But there was no response. I kicked a small rock that went skittering away.

Why did you do that?

I didn't say anything. I was annoyed that I was now faced with making a decision myself, something I had been going out of my way to avoid since the accident. Which was foolish, I knew, but I preferred being able to follow instructions and not being personally responsible for others. If I did what was required, it would all be fine.

Teena? Bastet broke into my thoughts. *Why haven't we started going towards the secondary site?*

What secondary site?

There is another site, a few hours away from here, Bastet answered.

How do you know? I asked suspiciously.

Lorrin talks to me a lot, they answered.

It felt like a rebuke, as if I didn't. But Lorrin was their person and I wasn't.

If we keep going, I began, thinking it through as I spoke to them, since there was no difference, *we're going to have to spend a night in an EST, an emergency tent.*

I don't mind.

What if there is another quake? I thought.

Will there be? Bastet asked. *It was scary when the outpost started shaking. I didn't know what to do and Lorrin wasn't there.*

I was sorry to have mentioned it when I heard their worries.

Probably not, I reassured, even though I had no idea.

·   ·   ·

I cycled as long as I could, but we indeed did not make it all the way to the secondary site before night began to fall.

I grumpily set up the EST and squeezed in with Bastet, who seemed to find it exciting. I suppose it was larger than their carrier, anyway.

Largely in silence, we had dinner and then went to sleep.

The next morning, I was eager to get going, but first I made us breakfast. We sat together and Bastet somehow started a conversation about the joys and annoyances of living in an outpost while we ate. It was getting less strange to talk to a cat.

When we were done, Bastet happily leapt into the carrier.

Thank you for breakfast, they said. *I hope we find Lorrin soon.*

There was something odd about this companionship or whatever it was between Bastet and me. I had anthropomorphized animals in the past, but this was not the same thing. Bastet was their own self.

It made me consider how much cats worry. Is it the same as with humans? I thought Bastet seemed worried, but I didn't know them that well. How much of it was my own projection?

Bastet and Lorrin were clearly very attached. I wondered how they had come to be together.

In a small part of my mind, an envy for such a connection was forming, even though I had, with great intention, pursued a solitary life.

•　　•　　•

The secondary site was not far from where we had slept, but there was a steep incline before we reached it, which reassured me that stopping for the night had been the correct choice.

As we descended, Bastet began to pester me about what I could see, since the window in their carrier pointed behind us.

There is a cycle track in the sand, I reported.

That could be anyone, they dismissed, not comforted by my observation.

I think I see an EST below. And I was not only saying it for Bastet's sake. In the distance, there certainly appeared to be a tent.

As we got closer, I was proved correct and there was a bike beside it, although something looked off about the scene.

"Hello!" I called through the radio as I got off my bike. "Specialist Lorrin? Are you there?"

There was a slight gasp over the radio and then, "Who is it?"

"This is Specialist Cardinal. I've been sent to find you."

"Bastet is with you! I'm in the tent."

I shuffled Bastet and I through the EST's small airlock and into the not particularly larger space inside.

Lying on the narrow bed, wearing the bottom half of their surface suit, was Specialist Lorrin. Their face was a sickly pale, with a fine sheen of sweat, their expression pinched in pain.

"Are you okay?" I asked as I sat down beside them, a clearly ridiculous question.

Lorrin answered, "I was injured in the quake."

What happened? Bastet asked, getting out of the carrier as I opened it and hopping onto the bed to lay down beside Lorrin, purring.

Lorrin shifted slightly to accommodate the cat, their hand resting on Bastet's back.

"I was on the slope collecting samples. I fell when the ground started shaking and rolled to the bottom. By the time it stopped, I was partially covered by rocks. There was a small tear in my surface suit, but I was able to get the patch on quickly enough." They indicated a spot on their right leg, the patch obvious now that it had been pointed out to me.

We were lucky, I thought not for the first or tenth or even hundredth time since I had moved to Mars, that we did not have to use the gas-filled suits anymore. The pressure suits maintained their integrity long enough for a patch in all but the most extreme circumstances.

"And you were able to get back in here? That was lucky."

"I suppose, but my bike is damaged, as well as my leg, and I couldn't get back to the outpost and I can't raise anyone on the radio. I'm glad the two of you showed up."

They started to scratch Bastet's neck and the cat looked up at them, closing their eyes for a moment. Then, Bastet leaned against Lorrin's hand and continued to purr.

My relief in locating Lorrin was short-lived, however. I went back outside to look at the bike, leaving Bastet and Lorrin to reunite.

I had been hoping, I suppose, that the damage was less than Lorrin had assumed. But that prospect was quickly dashed.

The front wheel was bent in a way that precluded any quick fix. And the casing that contained the chain, drivetrain, derailleurs, and related parts—and protected them from the Martian environment—was badly cracked.

So there was no way to go back on two bikes.

I reviewed my choices.

Since we could not contact Northern from here, at least one of us had to return to Outpost Mutch to let them know Lorrin was injured.

If the Lunae Planum base came back online, we might be able to contact them from here, but I wasn't certain of that.

I went back into the tent, half-hoping that, despite their situation, Lorrin might have an idea about what we should do.

·   ·   ·

I could stay behind, Bastet suggested. *Without my carrier on your back, Lorrin could ride behind you.*

No, Lorrin and I both replied quickly. With another human present, I found that I both spoke and thought my words to Bastet. Lorrin seemed to do the same.

My immediate worry was that Northern would not send someone back to get Bastet. Probably they would; the cat had an implant after all, making them a scientific novelty. But would they make the same effort as they would for Lorrin or me?

"I could go on my own," I said, "and make contact and arrange for you to be picked up here."

Was that a good idea? What if I didn't make it back to the outpost? Then what would happen to Bastet and Lorrin?

"I'm not sure there are enough rations," Lorrin worried. "How long would they take? Until they are able to spare a vehicle?"

I was ashamed to realize that I had not even thought of that part, but Lorrin was right.

"What if," I began, with only a half-formed thought in my mind, "we used the trailer on my bike?"

For what? Bastet asked.

"I could use parts from the trailer on your bike and maybe the back wheel..." my mind was moving quickly and I could see the parts coming together, forming a hybrid, Frankenstein's monster sort of trailer that would allow Lorrin to at least recline while I rode with Bastet on my back.

I was not sure I could do it, but a desperate wish to find a way to get all three of us back had taken over my thoughts.

Maybe, Bastet interjected, *it would work better if you moved the wheel to the right. And we used the bedding to make it more comfortable.*

Bastet came out with me. I attached them to my bike's environmental controls while I worked on the trailer, so they could see what I was doing and offer suggestions.

Aside from the wheel, they suggested a head rest, a seat belt system, and a diagonal position for Lorrin that would distribute their weight more evenly. Perhaps cats ought to be engineers.

I got in the trailer and leaned back when I was done, to see if it would accommodate Lorrin, who was of a similar size to me.

It worked fine, for which I was enormously grateful, but it was obvious that there would be no space for either of the tents, so we would need to go back without stopping.

I pulled up the map on my visor's right hand corner display. The return route to the outpost was a straight line from here, more or less, and just within the distance I felt comfortable travelling without sleeping.

·   ·   ·

We were halfway back , according to the visor display, and I was exhausted. It had taken more effort than I expected just to get Lorrin into their full suit and helmet and into the trailer. And now it had been four hours on the bike and the same again until we could expect to reach the outpost. I could feel my mind beginning to wander and I had to force myself to focus on the path before me again and again.

The sun had set, smaller than it appeared on Earth and with a blue tinge to the sky, and we would have to travel through the long Martian twilight and into the dark the rest of the way to the outpost. There was a light on my helmet, but it only illuminated a narrow path reaching a couple of metres in front of us.

Can you see where we're going? Bastet asked.

The light is fine, I answered, with only slight exaggeration.

It was a strain, though.

Not dark like on Earth, where there was, more often than not, light coming from somewhere. Without any light pollution, the Martian night was dark and the stars brilliant, though with so little atmosphere, they didn't twinkle.

"Are you okay, Lorrin?" I asked. The other scientist had shown signs of increasing pain and I was worried. Worried for them, of course, but also worried about what I would do if their condition worsened.

Mostly, I wanted to get to somewhere where I could turn over responsibility to someone else.

There was a mumble over the comms channel linking my suit with Lorrin's that I took as a positive sign.

It will be okay, Bastet said out of nowhere.

I didn't know if they were speaking to Lorrin or to me, but I answered anyway.

I hope so, I said, trying to focus on our path, while pushing aside the worry gnawing inside me.

• • •

"I can see the outpost," I said with deep relief, hoping it was not a mirage.

There was merely a grunt, which at least reassured me that Lorrin wasn't dead.

I had stopped twice during the night to check on them. They had developed a fever, but, without any pressurized shelter, I could not look at the wound directly to check for infection yet.

I hope it will be okay. Bastet had been comforting, but of no practical help.

I wasn't sure how to respond to them.

Not far now, I said.

• • •

The last hundred metres were the worst. I felt like we were barely moving and I was back in my dream of the lab, not being able to move or speak, just watching as the horror played out.

While we traveled, I had, for the most part, pushed aside the thoughts of what to do after we got to the outpost. Now that we were here, Lorrin's need for urgent treatment was weighing on me.

We need to get Lorrin inside, Bastet said firmly, echoing my own thoughts.

I know, it will be just a minute.

When we finally got into the airlock, tired from the trip and eager to do something practical for Lorrin, I fumbled as I started the exterior door closing and got off my bike.

Lorrin appeared unconscious through their mask and I tried to figure out what to do next.

I could take off our helmets and check to see if they were breathing. Then I would lift them up to carry them through the inner door.

Or I could drag the trailer in.

Not that, Bastet said firmly. *The trailer can't go in the outpost.*

Strictly speaking, they were right; the trailer was dirty and potentially contaminated.

It was also explicitly the rules. The bike and the trailer, any outdoor equipment, stayed in the airlock.

However.

Wouldn't I mostly likely further injure Lorrin if I tried to half-carry them all the way from the airlock to the bed? It had not been far to move them from the tent to the trailer to begin with.

Help them, Bastet hissed at me.

When the door opens, I tried to reassure them. *I know you're worried, but we can't do anything until we're inside and it's clean and there's pressure.*

Bastet did not reply.

The door took so long. I wanted to get on with this, figure out what help I could or could not offer Lorrin.

When it was open, I said fuck it, unhooked the trailer from my bike, and dragged it into the outpost without pausing to take our helmets off.

I closed the airlock door and turned my attention to Lorrin.

Helmets off first, mine and then Lorrin's. I checked to make sure they were still breathing.

I exhaled with a little relief.

I pulled off my gloves as I went to retrieve the medical kit.

Let me out!

I took off the pack as quickly as I could and opened it.

I dragged the trailer along with the medical kit into the sleeping area with Bastest on my heels.

Happy that Lorrin wasn't too large, I pulled them onto the bed and began to loosen their surface suit. I opened the medical kit and took out a thermometer strip, which I slapped onto Lorrin's forehead.

Bastet had followed me into the bedroom and jumped up on the bed and sat beside Lorrin's head.

Are they okay? What are you doing?

I left the surface suit top hanging open and pulled off the pants so that I could see the wound on their leg.

It was oozing and the skin was red and swollen and tight. I couldn't tell if there was a broken bone and I didn't want to make the injury worse by moving Lorrin's leg.

Is it bad?

A little bad, I said, trying to sound cheerful. I followed up with an, *It will be okay*, forcing a confidence I did not feel.

I needed help.

"Northern? This is Specialist Cardinal," I said into the radio, but received nothing but static in reply.

Breathe.

"Northern," I all but squeaked. As I looked at Lorrin lying on the bed the familiar, panicked feeling of not knowing what to do next poured into me.

There was no response from Northern.

Do something, Bastet pleaded.

I had gone through some medical training. What was the first step?

Look for Instructions. There was a reader in the medical kit.

I pulled it out and began to flip through, looking for a situation like this.

While continuing to try to contact Northern, I cleaned and bandaged Lorrin's wound and gave them a shot of antibiotics.

Finally, there was a burst of static.

"Specialist Cardinal? This is Northern."

"Northern, I'm here."

"Good to hear from you, Cardinal. Where are you?"

"Outpost Mutch. And I have Specialist Lorrin. They have an infected wound."

There was the slightest of pauses. "Where is the injury?"

"Their leg."

"What is their temperature?" And they went through a series of questions to assess Lorrin's condition.

At the end, they reassured me that further assistance, including a doctor, was on the way.

Can I stay here? Beside Lorrin? Bastet asked.

Of course, I said.

And they stretched out along Lorrin's arm, letting their head rest on their person's shoulder.

As I watched, I was struck again by their closeness and felt a certain envy for their relationship.

There might always be pain, but there could also be comfort.

· · ·

"Specialist Cardinal, the vehicle will arrive at Outpost Mutch in the next hour."

They're here?

Almost.

Okay. I guess. And I watched as they settled back into position, their head resting now against Lorrin's elbow.

· · ·

Is it today? It's today, right? Bastet was beside themself with excitement. It was a month later and Lorrin had responded well to treatment. So today they were being transferred from the medical center to the rehabilitation unit and Bastet would be able to go with them.

While Lorrin had been healing, Bastet had been living with me.

I had accompanied Lorrin and Bastet to the regional base and then on to Curie City because I had nowhere else to go while the outpost waited for repairs.

I didn't think I was going to stay, but once here, I remembered everything I had liked about living in Curie City before the accident.

When I thought about the marsquake and Lorrin, I knew there were different decisions I could have made, like thinking more about what supplies would be useful when we went looking for Lorrin. But despite that, Bastet and I had found them and brought them to safety.

Somehow, working together, it had been okay.

Bastet bumped by ankle with their head. I was going to miss having them around. I was sure that my quarters would feel empty without them.

We're leaving now, I reassured the cat. *It's time to get into your carrier.*

·   ·   ·

I knocked on the door before we entered, as Bastet called out, *We're here!*

"Come in," Lorrin said. They brightened up when they saw my companion.

"Bastet!" they cried, holding out their arms as Bastet leapt onto the bed, rubbing the side of their face against Lorrin's chest.

"Thank you so much for taking care of them," Lorrin directed at me, focusing on the cuddly furrball in their lap

"It was no problem at all, really," I said, suddenly awkward as I sat down in a chair near the bed.

Teena has been so nice, Lorrin.

"Bastet has been a lovely guest," I countered. "I was glad to be able to help."

"Will you be going back to Outpost Sagan?" Lorrin asked.

"No," I replied uncomfortably, embarrassed by how much time I had spent on this decision. "I liked it, but I think I was there for the wrong reasons. I've been offered a job at the UNSpace Research Facility. I used to work there."

"Were you there when that accident happened?"

Taken aback, I stuttered, "Y-yes."

Lorrin nodded. "I thought you looked familiar. I was working there at the time, too. Was it hard to decide to go back?"

I was quiet for a moment, not sure how to explain.

"Yes, it was," I finally said. "It was terrible, the accident. But then I went and lived remotely and look what happened."

Lorrin laughed.

"I won't be in the same part of the facility, but I think it's the right thing to do. I hope so, anyway." It helped to say out loud the words I had been repeating in my mind.

"I'm going there, too, after I finish therapy," Lorrin said. "The doctor said I should take it easy and not go back to a solo outpost quite yet."

"Maybe we'll see each other sometime," I said, unsure but hopeful.

"I'll treat you to lunch," Lorrin said firmly.

I smiled slightly. I quite liked Lorrin, I thought.

I like Lorrin, too, Bastet added.

You shouldn't eavesdrop, I said back.

Then I stood up. "I need to be going, I'm afraid."

Good bye, Bastet, I thought.

You need to stay in touch with me, too.

Of course, I said as I left.

As I headed back to my apartment, I felt the beginning of something that had been missing for a long time. A desire to spend time with others, to let go of the fear of what might happen, to learn to relax, if only a little, into the unknown.

CASE STUDY

Alice "Huskyteer" Dryden

Hypothesis

At the Velogalactic Company Limited (head office: Pluto), we constantly strive to understand and support the needs of our valued customers and potential future customers.

As Sales Manager, Outlying Minor Planets Division, I agreed to visit Planet K-137 and investigate, in the words of my line manager, "why the bloody cats aren't buying the bloody bikes."

K-137 is a horticultural planet, producing flowers and bulbs for interplanetary trade. The flower fields are irrigated by a network of canals.

The installed species is feline in form, created using genetic material from a number of small cats in the genus *Felis*, including the black-footed cat and the jungle or swamp cat. Referred to by traders as "tigerlilies," they were introduced to tend the flowers and control the various species of bird and rodent either native to the planet or inadvertently imported by visiting aliens.

Bipedal, they stand approximately one metre tall, with an average weight of around 30kg in Earth gravity. Males tend to be larger and heavier. The fur may be either a solid grey or rust color, or tawny with small spots. The ears are rounded. The pads of the paws, and surrounding fur, are black. A tail is present, as it is in many created species. Although no longer necessary for balance, it is simpler to leave the tail in place than to edit it out, and tails are also perceived as aesthetically pleasing.

(See figure 1, attached: Dave, with tail visible.)

The cats are solitary, with each individual patrolling a large territory. Their diet consists mainly of rodents and birds, supplemented by fish and frogs from the canals.

The flowers of K-137 are classed as a luxury item and grown under strictly controlled conditions. The use of pesticides is banned. Larger vermin are kept in check by the cats, and insect pests by predator species such as spiders and ladybugs. The flowers are pollinated by bees; looking after the beehives is another task assigned to the cats.

Solar or wind power, or hydroelectricity, is used to prevent pollution of the flower fields. Spaceships orbit K-137's moon with their engines powered off, and are loaded using water-powered elevators. Harvesting, the spreading of natural fertilizers, and other tasks are carried out by hand rather than using machinery, to enhance the luxury experience. Once harvested, the flowers are placed in sub-zero suspension for space travel—arriving, according to the current advertising campaign, "as fresh as the instant they were picked by kitten paws."

The environmental legislation of the planet, combined with the need of the cats to travel long distances as they carry out their work, would seem to make the inhabitants of K-137 ideal customers for the products of the Velogalactic Bicycle Company Limited (head office: Pluto).

However, sales proved sluggish, and I was determined to drive them up.

Method

I met Rush, my host, at her home in K-137's upper northern sector. She is 25 standard years of age, with reddish fur.

Insofar as the cats have a structured society, Rush is a local figure of some importance. As an area supervisor, she is responsible for ensuring that harvest quotas and quality standards are met; a role not dissimilar, perhaps, to a Sales Manager. I hoped that if I persuaded her to purchase one of our products, others would follow suit.

Rush welcomed me and we sat down to a meal of fish stew. (Since cats obtain all the nutrients they need from meat and fish, I took supplements during my stay to counteract the lack of grains and vegetables in my diet.)

I noticed there was little furniture in Rush's home. We dined sitting on mats woven from reeds, and later we would sleep on them.

In the night, I woke to find Rush draping a blanket over me.

"I forgot you don't have fur," she said.

The next morning, I introduced Rush to the Velogalactic Company Limited's latest model, the Photon. Combining an ultralight frame with convenient folding technology and all-terrain wheels, it is an excellent performer both on and off road. Our sales brochure describes it as "a joy to ride" and "built for both comfort and speed." Our salespeople, unofficially, describe it as "sex on wheels."

Rush had never ridden a bicycle before, but her feline sense of balance is acute, so she didn't require much teaching. We set off along one of the canalside paths to inspect the territory she covers. I was riding my own bike, an original Venus racer. Although the company encourages us to upgrade at a deep discount, I like the Venus and I have made a number of modifications to it over the years.

The lack of atmospheric pollution makes the sunlight on K-137 exceptionally pure and strong. The water glittered, and, to our right, fields of red and yellow flowers stretched to the horizon. In front of me, Rush cycled steadily, the sun turning her red-brown fur to gold and tracing a bright line around each hair.

The first problem became apparent almost immediately. Rush's tail, which swayed from side to side as she pedalled, came so dangerously close to getting trapped in the spokes of the rear wheel that I drew up alongside her and yelled at her to stop. She dismounted, ears flat and fur bristling, and I explained the issue.

I was able to improvise a guard for the rear wheel using a flattened drinks container and some wire. It spoiled the lines of the Photon rather, but that was better than spoiling the lines of Rush. We continued our ride, past windmills that cast whirling shadows on the flower fields. Sometimes we stopped so Rush could inspect the plants for signs of rodent infestation. I joined her as she walked through the lines of flowers, brushing against them; feline scent discourages pests. Pollen and petals decorated my clothes and her fur as we passed, and the foliage rippled with the wind or the passage of fleeing wildlife.

Towards the end of the morning, I noticed that Rush was tiring faster than I had anticipated. I pedaled alongside her so I could analyse her riding style.

A cat's forelimbs are almost as long as the hind, enabling them to travel on all fours when necessary or convenient. This meant that the handlebars and pedals were not in the optimum position for Rush to power the machine. I adjusted the handlebar height as far as I could, but it was still less than ideal. Furthermore, cats walk in digitigrade stance, like a human on tiptoe. Rush's hind paws did not fit the bicycle's toeclips, causing wasted effort on the upstroke of each cycle. This was something I wouldn't be able to fix with the portable toolkit I'd brought on the ride, but would have to wait for our return.

While I worked, Rush caught two fish in the traditional manner: by scooping them out of the canal with her paw. She killed and gutted them, and strung them on a pole for transport. This we attached to the rear carrier.

When the sun was at its highest point, we stopped for lunch. We chose a spot by a bridge, where Rush could sprawl out in the sun while I sheltered in the shade.

She cooked the fish in a solar-powered boiler. I suggested a barbecue, but that would fall foul of K-137's pollution laws.

"Well?" I asked. "What do you think?"

A tour of inspection that would ordinarily have taken all day had been completed in a couple of hours. I expected to find Rush full of praise for the Photon.

She twisted her head to lick a tuft of fur on her shoulder back into place, turned back and stared intently at me, her green eyes slightly crossed and the pupils narrow in the sunlight.

"Christine," she said, struggling to push the syllables through her canine teeth. "Why do the bikes have to be adapted for us? Why can't they be built for us in the first place?"

Conclusion

Please consider this my letter of resignation from the Velogalactic Company Limited (head office: Pluto).

I am happy to work my one month's notice period, or to take 28 days' paid gardening leave in accordance with company policy, before starting my new career as joint CEO of Rush Bikes Unlimited.

I undertake not to encroach on Velogalactic's sales territory, nor to use information or contacts gained during my employment against my former employer.

I have learned many valuable lessons from my time as Sales Manager, Outlying Minor Planets Division, and I plan to use these going forward as we create a client-centric organisation using a bottom-up approach.

Not everyone in the galaxy is humanoid in form, and rather than offering a one size fits all solution, we will recognize and celebrate the fact by designing from scratch for each and every life form.

You have your client base. We have ours. And ours offers infinite possibilities.

JETTA

Judy Upton

"Buying food again" the stallholder sneered at Jetta. "It's not as if you can even eat it." Jetta regarded him for a moment, and then lowered her electric blue eyes to pack her groceries. The man was not, however, done with her. "I don't know why you don't shop in the supermarket – where you'd be buying from your own kind." Jetta ignored the jibe. Unfortunately, she reasoned she had more in common with this prejudiced member of the human species than she did the automated tills to which he was referring. She forced her smile number two, the one optimistically designed to diffuse hostility.

"You don't happen to have any cat food, do you?"

The man cackled hoarsely.

"Cat food? Cat food it says? Your kind don't keep cats, 'cos your kind don't have feelings."

"Try telling that to Erasmus."

Erasmus had arrived with a collar disc bearing his name but no other details. For the first few weeks Jetta had tried to ignore him as she cycled around her beat, checking that burglar alarms, locked gates and barred windows were all doing their job. Erasmus was not, however, a cat to be ignored. He'd run along walls, stroll along walkways and barely give Jetta time to dismount before he was rubbing around her titanium legs, body throbbing with the deepest of purrs. When the owners of apartments in this upmarket suburb had decided the occasional police patrol was no deterrent to the criminals flooding in from the city's grimmer neighbourhoods, then they had clubbed together to hire her firm to provide them with surveillance drones and security androids. Erasmus must have originated in one of the luxury apartments and villas that Jetta watched over, but judging by his thinness and untreated wounds from a recent fight, he no longer had a home with the humans still living in it. A couple of times, Jetta had disturbed him sleeping out of the rain in a doorway or alcove. On the first occasion he had startled her she had almost shot him in error.

Officially Jetta wasn't armed, as the law forbade it, but money talked louder, and her company was extremely eager to please their affluent clientele. Jetta had no legal authority and was supposed to merely contact the police if she saw a burglary, carjacking or mugging occur. But everyone knew that the police were now so reduced in numbers by a city unwilling to pay higher taxes to stem its crime-wave that they would be highly unlikely to turn up at an incident. Jetta had no powers of arrest, and with only a bicycle as transport, no method of taking miscreants anywhere. What she did have was a completely steady aim, deadly accuracy, and, as her supplier insisted, no emotions.

Once a human target had been dispatched, her company would send a tidy crew to remove the body. In this neighbourhood, with its manicured lawns and swimming pools, it was quite normal to see kids walking about with a stiff-legged gait, pointing toy guns at each other and mimicking the sound of a silenced round or two. Most of them had actually witnessed an android shoot a criminal on their street or in their apartment block. It was a fact of daily life here—an open secret to which the local council and police turned a blind eye. Complaints to both organizations had fallen dramatically since Jetta and her colleagues had been deployed on the streets, and that was good enough for the authorities.

Jetta lived in a small concrete hut beside the air conditioning units, on the roof of one of the buildings she protected. It was also the roof the drones landed and left from, and she had to be careful not to collide with them as she took her folded cycle from the lift. Erasmus hated the drones and would hiss at the inanimate ones awaiting instructions, or rush past them, making a beeline for Jetta's hut, where he would greet her with purrs and leg rubs as she followed him inside.

Erasmus ate his food, crouched in front of the little dish Jetta had bought him. She had a payment card for essential purchases such as technical upgrades, hardware, cycle spares, and bullets, but in the market they still took cash, which was handy because by spending the coins and notes she found on those she had eliminated, she could keep her purchases of groceries and cat food a secret from the company.

The cat food had its purpose. The cat was hungry. It was a functional purchase. But Jetta did not fully understand why she bought human food items too. In her downtime, while charging her batteries, Jetta arranged and rearranged the packets and tins in her store cupboards and on her shelves. She found it interesting to arrange them in "sell by" date order one day, and then by weight or colour the next. It made no sense, but Jetta felt a compulsion to do it.

Cycling on her rounds, Jetta found herself still thinking about her groceries until the sound of a loud cry from around a blind corner clicked her mind back into work mode. A woman was sprawled on the ground, her mugger making a speedy getaway on a motorized skateboard. Jetta was programmed to respond to the criminal, not the victim, and would have sped in pursuit, had the woman not let out a moan of pain. Somehow, something in Jetta once again overrode her programming. Her role was to incapacitate or kill the robber, but instead she found herself dismounting her cycle and tending to the woman sprawled on the pavement.

"I'm broken too I think." Jetta admitted to Aneen a short time later as the woman bathed her own bloodied face. "I'm a crime bot, but I have a cat, I buy food from supermarkets and I helped you instead of carrying out my duties." Aneen looked at the chrome being reflected behind her in the mirror as its shiny arms made a shrugging gesture. "What's your cat called?" Aneen asked, as something to say. She'd never spoken to an android before and was slightly unnerved by the experience.

"Erasmus. I did not name him. It is on his collar. I did not know cats have human-given names, or that they answer to a name like I do." Trying to explain anything was awkward for Jetta. She was designed to report on crimes, to deal with facts and statistics. She'd discovered through talking to Erasmus that she could create complex sentences about other subjects, but it took her slightly longer.

Aneen looked at Jetta's silver face, currently showing its number three smile, and tried to see something in her expressionless, blue, glass eyes. Aneen had disapproved of the introduction of crime bots. To her it was too brutal a solution. A machine that gunned down starving people stealing to survive was a step too far. Still, she had to admit that this one had proved useful, coming to her aid and getting her back inside the safety of her home despite the theft of her entry card.

"Would you like a…" Aneen tailed off. She had been about to offer her guest her choice of beverage. It was daft; she was reacting to this bot as if it were human. Jetta could not drink tea or coffee. "Would you like to look inside my store cupboards?" she offered instead.

"Very much." Surely that was not enthusiasm she detected in the crime bot's voice?

"I have to keep my cat a secret, and my collection too," Jetta admitted as together they rearranged Aneen's store cupboard in date order, "or they'd have me in and reprogram me." Aneen nodded.

"Look, I know this is probably rude of me to ask, Jetta, but do you ever get lonely?"

"I think I did. Before I got Erasmus. Now it's fine."

"Only... I mean I work from home for a big corporation" Aneen explained, "And often I don't have a conversation–a real conversation from one day to the next..." Jetta nodded in her slightly formal way.

"Yes, I understand. You need a cat." At that, Aneen started and sighed.

"No, Jetta, I..." But Jetta had already risen and was heading for the door.

"Now I must hunt down your attacker. But tomorrow I will bring you a cat." Jetta knew there were lots of strays in the dilapidated slum she must visit to dispatch Aneen's mugger. She would easily find her a cat. Then Aneen would be fine.

"Look" said Aneen, "Forget about the mugger okay? He probably needs the money from my purse more than I do." Jetta didn't hear her. Her programming had prioritized dealing with Aneen's assailant over anything else. "But Jetta, I... I really don't want you hunting down this man..." Aneen heard the front door click shut. Jetta had already gone.

Across town, the family of the man who had mugged Aneen were making preparations. They knew the android's software would have immediately compared its recorded footage of the young man to its database. Masks, hoods and other disguises were no deterrent to an algorithm that could identify individuals by their tiniest movement. It was a slight surprise the crime prevention droid had not already turned up. Perhaps its batteries had been too low to allow it to make an immediate pursuit and kill. Still, it meant they were now ready for it. It had cost the family a lot of credits, and put them in debt with even more dangerous people, but now they were the first in their slum to own a metal-melter cannon.

As Jetta honed in on the dilapidated block where her target lived, her sensors alerted her to a massive energy surge in the vicinity. As she turned her head to try to locate its source, the last thing she saw was a huge blast of pure white heat hurtling towards her, before her arms and legs were ripped off by the force of the blast, her torso bending and collapsing in on itself as it melted. Pieces of bicycle shrapnel flew across the slum, embedding themselves in walls and shattering any previously un-smashed windows.

Aneen looked sadly at the brand new dish bearing the word 'cat' and the packet of luxury food for felines that she had purchased, along with a top-of-the-range cat bed and scratching post. It had been three days since she had been mugged and the android had still not returned. Resigning herself to a continued life of isolation, Aneen went to bed.

Two nights passed. Then suddenly the door scanner bleeped, waking Aneen from her slumber. She rubbed her eyes and summoned the door scanner image to her phone. It was 4am, and Jetta was standing outside. Aneen rushed to let her in. "I am late. I had to rebuild myself." To Aneen, Jetta didn't look any different, apart from perhaps being even slightly shinier than when they'd first met. "I did not need to reboot all of my circuits, so I remembered this." Jetta held out a cardboard box that had once contained soup cans and was now pierced with air holes. "I found you a cat," she said. "It's only my data bank of crime files that was corrupted. Was I on a mission when I left here?"

"Only to find me a cat," Aneen told her, not wanting to remind Jetta that she had actually been heading out to kill someone. "Can I see him or her?"

As Aneen cautiously opened the flaps, a blurred black and white shape leapt out and disappeared behind the sofa.

"She just needs time to get to know you." Jetta explained, "Then you won't be alone."

Aneen watched as Jetta turned to leave. She wanted to say something, to tell this robot that she was grateful for the cat, but she would also like company of a different kind, not human exactly, but someone she could have a conversation with from time to time. Now that Jetta could no longer remember the deadly mission she had been programmed for, perhaps that might be possible.

"Jetta I..." Aneen hesitated. "Jetta, I know we put my store cupboard in date order the other day, but I'm wondering if maybe it would be better to rearrange the packets by shape or colour?" Jetta paused in her tracks, then turned back, glass eyes almost seeming to glow. "Yes," she said. "Let's do that now, Aneen."

THE TIGER'S TALE

Juliet Wilson

Centuries ago, my ancestors roamed in great numbers in the jungles of a whole continent. Then bipeds hunted them to extinction.

I was cloned by the bipeds when they started to feel remorse for how they had devastated an entire planet.

I was lonely. I explored every inch of my tree-filled enclosure, but even with all the beautiful flowers it wasn't enough. I could feel the tug of endless jungles filled with tasty animals. I tried to ignore it. After all, I didn't know if there were any jungles left. I was alive, that had to be enough, the first of my kind to be alive for centuries. I delighted in my orange fur, my stripes, the white patches on my ears, and my roar that reverberated through the other enclosures, terrifying the various cloned animals in the menagerie. I loved to whisk my tail and call storms down on the bipeds if they didn't feed me enough.

My life changed the day my tail failed to bring down a storm when I needed one.

I barely heard a whisper in the grass before something hit me in the side and I fell.

"There she goes!" a biped whispered. Three of them gathered around me. I tried to move my tail but it was paralyzed. As were my paws. I felt my eyes closing. Sound faded away.

When I awoke, I was here. It took me several minutes to get used to the low light. I was lying on a thin layer of hay and straw that barely covered the metal beneath. The air was musty and metallic. Strange whirring and throbbing sounds filled the enclosed space. I raised a paw and licked it. It tasted dusty. I roared but I sounded like one of those domestic cats that hunted mice and submitted to petting from the bipeds.

I didn't want to think about my tail.

I must have fallen asleep because the next thing I remember was being poked as a biped pushed a plate of smelly meat substitute under my nose.

"Eat this!" she said. "You need to build your energy up! It's a long journey to Mars and you're the future of your species!"

I roared in disbelief but still sounded like a domestic cat. The biped smiled.

"Yes, you are an important cat!" she said, stroking my head.

I tried to move my tail but it felt as though it was tied to the metal floor.

Over the next few days the same biped visited me with meat substitute.

"This is a spaceship. There isn't much room, I know. The battery of cyclists takes up so much space, but we can't have you mixing with the other animals." She stroked the top of my head between my ears. I snarled, but she only laughed. "You're beautiful when you're angry!" she continued. "And just wait! It will all be wonderful when we get to Mars!"

Her voice was soft as she explained about the biped settlement on Mars, which had terraformed part of the planet. Now they were introducing animals from earth. I was to be the mother of a new population of my kind. I should be proud, she told me as she tickled me under the chin.

When she left I redoubled my efforts with my tail. I could feel the magic starting to return. A swish rocked the ship slightly. I purred. My voice was stronger now.

It was a week before I was able to call down a small storm. Thunder sounded over the endless whirring of the cyclists in the battery. The ship rocked from side to side. I purred again.

The next week I worked on conserving my energy and building up my anger. I didn't eat. I wanted the bipeds to think I had used up all my powers in calling the small storm. I didn't make a sound when the biped petted me, tears in her eyes as she pleaded for me to eat again.

When I felt electricity building in the base of my tail, I slowly stood up, whisked my tail through the dusty cabin, and roared.

Definitely not a domestic cat.

The spaceship vibrated with my sound. It rolled from side to side. A sound like thunder crashed through the corridors. The cyclists screamed as they were thrown to the floor. The wiring sparked like lightning from one end of the ship to the other. Molten plasma flooded through the engine room.

I would not be a pawn in the destruction of another planet. I roared again.

LIKE A CAT NEEDS A BICYCLE

Kiya Nicoll

"You know I don't approve of that contraption. Split skirts and nonsense."

Audrey tucked the parcel under her arm. "It makes it much more efficient, ma'am, to bring things to the clients, and they pay for service."

Mrs. Godfrey sniffed. "I suppose I oughtn't expect anything else from a suffragette. So long as you don't inflict any of your political nonsense on the clients."

"Of course not, ma'am."

"Who's this for, then?"

"The country girl who wanted the Eastern Continental, slightly conservative, for occasions."

"The green then, in the rational dress style." She nodded thoughtfully. "No accounting for taste. Final payment?"
Audrey shook her head. "Final fitting, ma'am. So I can have the adjustments done for her to pick it up Monday."

"Can't she come in for a fitting?" Mrs. Godfrey's clients tended to be the sorts of women who had free mornings or an hour before teatime. "You could try to convince her to adjust to something a little more fashionable."

"She's a working girl, ma'am, I told her I'd bring it around the house she tends and get it done after hours."

The senior seamstress shook her head. "Well, on with you, then. And be prompt in the morning, I've Mrs. Evanston coming in to fuss about embroidery. She claims if a single stitch is out of place it will ruin the 'magic' so I have to plan the entire morning to deal with her tosh. At least rich people pay for their nonsense, is all I can say."

"Yes, ma'am." Audrey took the dress out to the back, tucked it into her bicycle pannier, and angled out and down the edge of the road. It was a fairly straight shot to the address she was given, which was on a little street of fenced gardens and brick houses. She walked her bicycle inside the correct yard, left it to lean against the fence next to the gate, and went to the kitchen entrance to rap politely on the door and apologize for the lateness of the hour.

She took the measurements for a perfectly ordinary fitting, with the addition of a nice cup of tea. It was very late indeed by the time she was leaving and the Fog was thick enough that she paused to light the alchemical lamp on the bicycle, not wanting to trust the gas lamps to find her way. At least there was very little foot traffic to interfere, and only a few carriages, steam or horsedrawn, to dispute the use of the streets.

"Ayow," greeted her, in quite querulous tones, when she opened the door to her flat.

"Terribly sorry," she answered the cat. "It was rather a day."

The grey queen twined around her ankles and let out a more plaintive sound.

"Are you hungry, then? I suppose you're a good enough ratter to run out of mice, aren't you? Come on, I've got a bit of roast I can share." It was a pleasant enough fancy, that they could talk like old friends sharing rooms, and certainly the creature was often inclined to hold up her end of the conversation.

The cat trilled and followed her towards the kitchen, tail quirked and arcing gently at the tip.

"My day? Why, thank you for asking, Grimalkin." Audrey ran a hand over the cat's head as she hopped up onto a chair. "Mrs. Godfrey disapproves of everything, including the bicycle, but we knew all that already. I'm lucky that I'm very good, or she'd sack me and find a nice girl who doesn't know how to see to the rational dress types, and then where would she be? Half her clients gone like a puff of Fog."

"Prrrt," said Grimalkin somberly.

"You're quite right. We'd all be in a pickle if she did, so a good thing she doesn't. Oof, I'll need to be sending a note 'round to the iceman to drop off some extra when he makes the house delivery, we'll lose our chill soon. And the ice chamber's got your fur in it somehow."

"Prrrow?"

"No, it's too late to go for a ride right now. There you go." She set the plate down, and the cat stood up, forepaws on the table, to inspect it before peering at her. "No, go ahead, I have to set up the mannequin."

"Prt?"

Audrey leaned up in the doorframe, starting to undo the parcel. "This girl I'm making a dress for, I don't know what to make of her. She's some sort of lady's companion, I suppose, says she's doing scientific research on the side, of all things."

The cat blinked slowly, then grabbed a piece of the roast with one paw and snapped her jaws on it.

"Precisely. She told me she hadn't given a moment's thought to the vote! Honestly." She had the dress unwrapped, and started setting it up on the mannequin in the other room. "Even with her friend, who's a lady alchemist, having the devil of a time with publication with no man to take credit for it." She yanked on the dress firmly, taking care not to damage it. "I certainly hope she'll think about it, though. I gave her the card for the temperance house."

Grimalkin made a noncommittal noise and took another scrap of meat, hopping down off the chair with it and oozing past Audrey on her way to the bedroom.

"Well, fine, then, I shan't tell you any more about my day!" Audrey called after her. "Should I have enquired about yours?"

The cat, being a cat, did not respond, so she set herself to putting the dress on the dummy and pinning it in accord with the notes she had taken at the evening's fitting. At least the adjustments were easy enough to do before bed, so the dress could go back to the shop in the morning before Grimalkin turned any of it grey with shed fur. She took a light supper and went to bed, the cat eventually deciding to curl up in the small of her back.

Morning brought a simple breakfast, including a bit of cat's meat for Grimalkin, and the cat looking hopefully at the door. Audrey rubbed her between the ears and said, "Not right now, lovie, I have work. I need to be in on Saturdays, for all the working girls, don't I? I'll see if Lillian has some ice to spare on the way home, to tide us over until Monday."

Grimalkin was still sulking when she left, washing her face with a sullen, ears-canted-back aggravation after she had been shoved back from the door twice so Audrey could leave. "Later, lovie!" she called through the door, then hurried down to tuck the finished dress into the pannier and start rolling towards the shop.

Audrey brought the bicycle into the back of the shop like usual, putting it out of the way and unloading the parcel.

"What's all this then?" demanded Mrs. Godfrey, one hand on her hip.

Audrey ignored the implications of the statement and answered the question in a way that was likely to go somewhere useful. "The dress for the country girl, ma'am, all packed up and ready for her to collect."

As she had hoped, the diversion worked. "What, you've done the alterations already?"

"Last night after I saw her. It was just a few things I could do right away. Better not to spend the time here on something so easy."

Mrs. Godfrey grunted. "I suppose you're likely to have a busy day of temperance girls and trade unionists."

"Being a working girl doesn't mean a lady can't appreciate bespoke," Audrey said, with as much politeness as she could muster, but the elder seamstress was already turning away.

It turned out to be a reasonably busy day. Saturdays often were, particularly after lunch, when the people who got off early were hurrying about to do the errands that relied upon the people who did not. She had a meeting with a trade unionist who was looking for a smart jacket, a shop girl with a friend who had a number of strong opinions, two temperance ladies who had been to three shops already and bickered with the seamstresses there, and an embarrassed young lady who confessed to needing something in split skirts for a bicycle. Mrs. Godfrey entertained the more conventional clients she preferred, in more leisurely intervals between cups of tea. Come closing time for the shop, the senior seamstress said, "What'd you get done, then?" and Audrey listed off her accomplishments, in good order and with proper attributions to each client.

"All right then. I suppose you can take Monday after all. What was it you were doing?"

"Mrs. Nelson—a friend of my mother's—she's ailing, and we take turns to sit with her, ma'am." It was true enough, even if the old lady was also a fine and pointed agitator providing instruction to the younger generation, but that answer would neither get her the time nor leave her reliably in possession of a good situation.

"I suppose that's a properly diligent thing to be doing." It was grudging, but that was expected. "And you'll be back Tuesday?"

"Yes'm. It's Alice's turn Tuesday. My cousin."

"Go on with you, then."

Audrey nodded and escaped into the back, dragging the bicycle down the back step and setting off with an irritated kick. She made her escape, feeling the wind in her face even with the Fog, and the sense of freedom that came of simply being able to go where she wanted, even if she must mind the muck from the horses and dodge the occasional steam carriage. There was certainly time to visit Lillian and see if she could get some ice.

She propped the bicycle up near the door for servants and tradesmen and knocked.

"Audrey! I wasn't expecting you!" Lillian was a bit younger, but entirely enthusiastic about the vote when she had the time away from work, which was not often. "You didn't happen to bring that moggy of yours around, I might have a bit of a treat for her."

"Afraid not, came by straight from work." Audrey stepped into the back hall and out of the Fog.

"That's a shame, then. I know she likes it when you take her out. Such an odd thing, a cat riding a bicycle." She shook her head. "So what brings you, then?"

"Terribly sorry, I know it's Saturday, but I was wondering if Mr. Golden's run his engine recently and there was a bit of ice I might buy off him? My icebox is a bit scant and the iceman won't come 'round to supply the flats until Monday."

"Oh, he won't sell on a Saturday." Lillian gestured her into the kitchen. "Spot of tea? You really should've brought Grimalkin, I'd have a coin for two hours of a decent mouser right now."

"Still no luck figuring out where they're coming in?"

"Not a bit." The kettle was on already and steaming gently, and Lillian poured out a cup. "Do you know what's wrong with your icebox, then?"

"No notion. It seems to be in working order, it just, well. It's unpredictable. I've no idea why sometimes it takes the notion to half-melt all in one go."

"You should have someone come 'round to look at it."

"Probably ought," she agreed with a sigh, and had a sip of tea. "So, the ice? Do you think I might?"

Lillian glanced towards Upstairs and then back with a grin. "Well, if I did a bit of business for him it'd be all right. I've done it before. And he did run the engine yesterday to make a batch of his fancy alchemical coal. If you replace your icebox, do you suppose you might get an alchemical one? I've heard they're quite reliable."

"Not on my wage, I won't. That's silk money and I'm afraid I'm a linen sort of girl."

Lillian nodded solemnly. "Well, at least ice is getting cheaper," she said. "One way or another."

They spent a while talking over their tea. Eventually Audrey bought a block of ice, writing a note to thank the alchemist for the indulgence, and she and Lillian got it loaded into the bicycle pannier. "Next time be sure to bring the cat around. She's so well-behaved. Better than half the lap dogs I've met."

It was again dark enough for the lamp, and Audrey paused under a streetlamp to make certain the bicycle was in proper order before setting off along the dim evening streets, unconfined by the need to be answerable to a cab or a trolley schedule. She made a brief stop at the corner shops for necessities, loaded them into the other pannier, and then skimmed gaily the rest of the way home and hauled the bicycle inside to sit in the vestibule with the others. Getting the ice and tomorrow's meat to her flat seemed to take longer than the ride back had done, for all that it was a far shorter trip, without the breeze tugging back at her hat and the sense that a dozen yards of accomplishment could be had in a single step.

"Quarter of the way across Camlon in a breath and it takes a lifetime to get up the stairs," she muttered, as she opened up the door to the flat. Grimalkin made no attempt to escape; it turned out that she was curled up on top of the icebox, sleeping, her paw resting on a tatty bit of ribbon that she had somehow twisted in a loop around it. "Aren't you supposed to look for warm places to nap?" Audrey asked, as she opened it up to see how difficult it would be to wedge in the new ice slab.

The cat yawned, stretched, and sat, blinking at her curiously as she swept out the detritus in the ice drawer with a rag and popped the new block in with a, "Nothing but fur, we'd have had spoilage by morning without."

Grimalkin blinked lazily, then hopped down and twined around her ankle before trotting towards the door. She looked back expectantly and made a little hopeful trilling noise.

"No, we're not going out, I've only just got back in, silly creature." Audrey set about preparing herself dinner. She set out a dish for the cat, who eventually slunk back in, shot her a rather dark look, and ate her offal with her ears slanted back before retreating to the corner to wash her face with obvious irritation. There was in the end very little to be done about a sulky cat, so Audrey left her to it, cleaned up, and retreated to the bedroom to practice some embroidery until she felt it was a good time to sleep.

The thump awakened her in the middle of the night, and Audrey fumbled for the striker to light the lamp and grabbed a pair of scissors from the side table. Lamp in hand, scissors held like a weapon, she edged slowly to the bedroom door and peered out to identify the intruder.

"Grimalkin!"

The cat looked up at her, a trailing end of a ribbon in her jaws, and gave it a firm shake, like she might a snake, before trotting over and dropping it at her feet.

"How much have you ruined, you ridiculous beast," Audrey said, scooping it up and inspecting it. Several punctures, but mostly towards the end, and as she respooled it she smoothed it out to make certain she had not missed anything. "How on earth did you get into that?" She kept the ribbons in a chest of drawers that latched, precisely because the cat could not be trusted and in fact had to be shut into the bedroom whenever the ribbons were out. One of those drawers, however, had been pulled entirely out and was presumably the source of the thump that had brought her out of bed.

"Mrowrl," the cat declared, rather querulously.

Audrey put the ribbon away, peered under the furniture to make certain none of the rest had been tucked away for further mischief, and carefully double and triple-checked the latches on the drawers. "I haven't been in there for over a week," she pointed out. "It's not like I could've left it unlatched this evening for you to get into."

Grimalkin blinked at her and started to clean her whiskers.

"At least nothing needs replacing." She stomped back into the bedroom to go, rather irritably, back to sleep. Morning came too early for an interrupted night, and Grimalkin did not help matters any by demanding to be fed at first light.

The owner of the block of flats was adamant that the residents should attend Sunday services, lest someone take the place—largely let to unmarried working women—as a house for the other kind of working girl. Audrey did not actually mind, not as much as some of the others. This morning, though, the interrupted night had her entirely out of sorts, and Grimalkin persisted in making matters worse, particularly when she darted out past Audrey's ankles and pattered down the stairs to the vestibule when she was trying to leave. "Cat loose! Mind the door!"

Rather than trying to make her escape or get into one of the other flats, Grimalkin had climbed up to the bicycle pannier, balanced precariously as she worked one paw under its lid, and slipped inside, to curl up, quite contentedly, in the expectation that she might go on a journey. Audrey scooped her out by the scruff, and lectured her firmly all the way back up to the flat, shoving her quite unceremoniously back inside before latching the door. "It's not even like I'm taking the bicycle!" she exclaimed to the affronted stripey back. "Next I go out I swear I shall leave you behind, even if Lillian did ask after you."

The church was just a little way down the street, and the lot of them trundled out of the rooming house, done up in their better clothes. They traipsed their way to the church in a group, chaperoned by the landlady, who made an ostentatious count and then led them off accordingly.

It was of course not the done thing to complain about the indignity of being treated like children in need of guidance, and so Audrey did not do it. During the service, she tried to set it aside in the spirit of forgiveness, more or less, and on the way back had managed good enough spirits to ask if any of her neighbors fancied coming over for a bit of lunch and some tea.

They settled themselves in the main room of the flat, and out came Grimalkin from the kitchen, with a curious, "Prrrrrt?" Nancy tried to convince her to hop up into her lap, but Harriet had more luck dangling a handkerchief down the side of her chair to get her attention.

"She's not much for laps," Audrey said, as she brought the tea out. "Only on her terms."

Nancy plucked up her teacup. "I'd rather a dog, then."

"I don't have time to cosset a beast," Harriet said, flicking her handkerchief at the cat again. "The amount of primping and fussing fancy ladies put into their lap dogs, it's practically a job all on its own. Just another way of showing themselves idle. A cat earns his keep, and so do I." She was, as always, tightly laced up with a high-collared white shirt under her shawl and dark skirts that would certainly show the cat hair if Grimalkin took the notion of rubbing on them.

Nancy considered, sipping at her tea. "I would like, then," she said, carefully, "to be fancy enough to have time for a lap dog." Nancy was, Audrey knew, quite pleased with the one silk petticoat she had managed to salvage from some cast-offs in a shop, and it had given her notions.

Harriet laughed. "There's the truth of it," she agreed.

Audrey set out the sandwiches. "Not that there's much chance of that for the likes of us."

"Not without the vote," Nancy said.

"Even with the vote," Harriet interjected. "Oh, there goes the cat."

"She'll be back soon enough, I imagine. If you want to bring her out, here." Audrey rummaged in a desk drawer and fetched out a few mismatched buttons and some tiny wooden spools, long since threadless, and set them on the table.

Harriet picked up one of the buttons, peered at it, and tossed it out onto the floor.

Grimalkin darted out from the bedroom, paws landing on the button and skidding over the boards, and the women laughed. It would make for an entertaining time, at least, and a diversion from politics and work and other frustrations, to toss things for the cat. When, after spending a bit of time batting one of the spools between quick grey paws, Grimalkin carefully knocked it under the skirts of a chair and came back to wait for the next, Nancy asked, "What's she doing?"

Audrey shrugged. "She likes to hide things away. Every few days I have to go under all the chairs and everything and see what she's made off with. Handkerchiefs and stockings, odds and ends."

Nancy laughed. "Well, let's see what she wants to keep and what she leaves out, why don't we?" And that started a run of rummaging through handbags to see what sorts of things won Grimalkin's approval.

In the end, the cat stole Harriet's handkerchief, a crocheted button with a pattern that looked like a cartwheel, and a half a walnut shell that Nancy had found in the bottom of her bag. While they watched Grimalkin trot around with the shell in her mouth, making yowling sounds of triumph, Nancy said, "Speaking of walnuts, I had a most curious customer the other day."

"Curious in what way?" Harriet asked, idly twitching a bit of ragged thread for Grimalkin's attention.

"So he comes in, and he's," she considered the words carefully. "Eccentric. One of those sorts with pockets full of all sorts of brass instruments, you know? Fancy eyepiece with dials on it, hanging on a chain. That sort of thing."

"What were his clothes like?" Audrey felt that a proper portrait of the peculiarity was required for a proper story, and besides, knowing the cut of the man's outfit was of professional interest.

"Yellow waistcoat, patterned with red," Nancy said immediately. "So he knows a dyer who gets the best alchemical dyes, or it was brand new, it wasn't mucked up from Fog smoke at all. I don't know fabrics by eye, Audrey, you know. But he had money, nothing at all shabby."

Audrey grinned. "Still, yellow waistcoat says a bit about the man, doesn't it? Odd enough to be so brash, and money for laundering too."

"If you say so," said Harriet.

Nancy tossed a button, but Grimalkin was still too pleased with her capture of the nutshell to do more than bat it back with a desultory paw. "He pulls this little metal lump out of his pocket and says he needs five walnuts, each one precisely that weight."

"He what?"

"I said he was strange, didn't I?" She shook her head. "He said he'd pay a ludicrous markup for it, so what can I do but spill out a half-basket of walnuts and start weighing them against his miniature paperweight? And I told him it was a right odd thing he was after, I'd never heard of a recipe calling for such a precise weight of unshelled walnuts, and he laughed at me."

"Well I never. Laughed at you for what?" Harriet was rather predictably outraged, enough so to stop trying to lure the cat.

"He said that obviously someone like me couldn't begin to understand the, what was the phrase? The 'niceties of the arcane arts', I think. And seemed to think I was quite the silly little girl for imagining he might want walnuts to cook with."

"What on earth is that supposed to mean?" Audrey asked, baffled.

"It means he's a magician, and right full of himself," said Harriet. "Doing some sort of fancy spell, I imagine."

"A magician, of all things." Nancy was, quite clearly, having none of it.

"They're quite the fashion in certain circles." Harriet shrugged and went back to flicking the thread.

"What, like table-knockers and spiritualists?"

"I expect they would consider themselves far too sophisticated for spiritualism, for the most part. It's all mathematics and calculations and drawing diagrams and having arguments with other magicians about how many points the star in the circle is supposed to have."

"How on earth do you know what magicians do, Harriet?" Audrey asked.

Harriet laughed. "You recall, I think it was two governess positions ago, I mentioned that the man of the house was difficult, though not the horribly difficult sort of difficult? One of the problems was the children had figured out how to pick the lock to his study and kept smudging his chalk diagrams. He was quite," she put on a mocking, deeper voice, "'Miss Reynolds you must understand that the practice of magic requires precision and care, and I cannot be having the children upending my candlesticks.'"

Nancy laughed. "Oh, that's much the same as the man in my shop, with the fussing over the precise weight of his walnuts. A magician, you say?"

"I would think he ought to have been more upset that upending his candlesticks might set a fire," Harriet noted. "But rich men are terribly impractical, really."

"There you go dashing my hopes of getting a lap dog."

They all laughed, and then Harriet gestured towards Grimalkin. "Look at her, though. Sorting through buttons and things and only taking the ones that suit, just like Nancy's wizard."

"I shan't let her have any candles," Audrey said. "The smell of scorched fur is utterly dreadful." At that, they moved the conversation to other topics, for a little while. Eventually she was left alone with Grimalkin, who had stashed her nutshell away somewhere and settled on one of the vacated chairs, one paw holding down her own tail so that she might lick it into submission.

"I suppose you've gotten your exercise," Audrey said, and the cat looked up at her, and then went back to grooming. "I shall work on making a Sunday roast so I have cold roast for the week, and then I shall read a novel."

Grimalkin blinked and curled up for a nap.

By the time she had the roast sorted out, the cat had moved to the top of the icebox once more, and stayed there for much of the remainder of the afternoon. She seemed, if anything, to be adopting an expression of ferocious concentration and Audrey left her to it. After supper, the cat spent rather a lot of time chasing nothing in particular up and down the flat, before withdrawing to the bedroom in advance of Audrey realizing that there were puddles and pawprints everywhere from the water that had leaked out of the icebox. Perhaps she would have to replace the thing after all.

After cleaning it all up, Audrey had been hoping for an uneventful sort of night, but sometime in its depths she was awakened by the cat yanking vigorously at her hair. She swatted the creature and snarled something quite unladylike, and Grimalkin fled, her feet thumping and sliding across the floor. "And stay out!" she said, and shut the door. "You're a terrible roommate, sometimes."

Early Monday morning, the cat was yelling, and she put a pillow over her head and ignored it until silence fell once more. She was not sure how long it was before the noise resumed, but eventually it became unignorable, dragging her out of the bedroom and into the front of the flat where she could see what Grimalkin had done.

She had certainly done a great deal. It appeared that several of the kitchen herbs had been uprooted from their pots and their leaves and dirt scattered from the kitchen into the parlor, for one, making a grand arc of ruination that curved around a space roughly defined by some knit stockings. "Grimalkin, have you been stealing my clothes again?" Audrey said, as she started to scoop them up. "Oh, ugh, did you make yourself sick chewing on my herbs?"

The center of the heap of stockings contained the crocheted button and the walnut shell, both lightly coated with a damp blob of grey fur mingled with crushed greenery and several long brown hairs that the cat must have pulled from Audrey's head, and a ribbon that trailed from the soggy mass out and over the stockings. Audrey sighed and went to get a rag to clean it up. "Honestly, I was hoping to sleep in a little before I went to visit Mrs. Nelson."

"Mrrrr?" The cat was seated on a cushion that she had pulled off a chair, as if she required a specially prepared box seat to observe her destruction.

"I shall have to see if I can salvage the button, it's a perfectly good button," she scolded. "And the stockings shall have to be washed, of course." Scooping up the refuse, she plucked the button out. "I rather like the style, honestly. It looks like a bicycle wheel."

Grimalkin made a noise which she fancied was rather like assent and scrubbed at her face with one paw.

"Of course if that's a bicycle wheel, then the shell could be one of my baskets, couldn't it? And the ribbon a bit of road. I'm cross with you about the ribbon, mind, though at least there's not much of it." She laughed. "I'm quite fanciful this morning, aren't I? Come on, no lasting harm done, I think, I'll put the plants to rights. Here we go."

The cat followed her into the kitchen and sat to one side, tail folded around her forepaws quite primly.

"And here's your breakfast, and now I'll make mine. And once I've done I'll see if Lillian would like your company for the day to scare the mice out of the Goldens' larder. I'm sure if you do a proper job of it she'll let you steal a bit of poor Mrs. Golden's headache tea, the one with the catnip."

Grimalkin blinked at her, and then went to wolf down the bit of meat she'd been given.

When Audrey opened the door to the flat, the cat started off down the stairs immediately, proud as a queen and just as secure in her command of her little world. By the time her human had made it down to the ground floor she had wriggled her way into the bicycle pannier and curled up there, with the sort of smug satisfaction known most particularly to cats.

"Silly creature," Audrey said, and rolled the bicycle out into the grey haze of the morning.

CONTACT IN 4, 3, 2, 1

Gerri Leen

The ship smells metallic after the rich scents of Earth. Padding on feet unused to artificial gravity—the humans don't notice the difference, but you certainly do—you head for the cockpit.

You ignore the calls of Hernandez and Po in the galley. This is normal behavior, established over centuries. Humans call; cats don't come. If they wanted obedience, they should have brought a dog.

"Fluffy, come here, sweet girl."

Fluffy. Your coat is plush, not long. You refuse to look at them, even if they have decided this is your name.

Of course, technically, the humans didn't bring you. You're of the wayfarer line. It's been the custom of your family to explore boundaries, to test the limits of what humans are capable of. Your ancestors rode on wagons, on ships, on the back of camels, even. You explored by train and car and airplane and now this spaceship.

You snuck aboard and hid in the part of the cargo hold where experiments are kept safe from changing conditions. Wasn't the crew surprised to see you? You acted scared, of course. Any simple beast would.

And it made them feel sorry for you. It gave you access to the entire ship.

It ensured you'd be *The One*. It's the greatest honor of your family, possibly of all of your kind.

It is also a privilege, and for a moment you let pride sink away and just enjoy doing something this good for so many.

Still, you know you're strutting as you enter the gym with your ears perked and your tail straight up, but it's more than just pride—in the most basic way possible, it tells the human you're about to come into contact with that you welcome interaction with her.

And she understands your kind enough to know it, leaning almost precariously off the exercise bike and holding her hand down for you to sniff and scent-mark. "Fluff, how's it going?"

You give her the short miaow that your kind would know means anticipation and she laughs as she always does when you converse with her.

Captain Lassiter is your favorite and not just because she's in charge. She never picks you up, instead gives you the chance to come to her, and she always laughs when you jump on her while she exercises.

As you do now, trying not to claw her as you make your way to her shoulder. Trying, but failing.

"Ow, Fluff. What I put up with." Despite her words, she's sitting up straight so you won't fall once you find your perch, and petting you just the way you like—leaning her head into you because she's told you she loves the sound of a purr drumming into her head.

Normally, she would be hunched over, legs pumping and breathing hard. You think cuddling up to you is much more pleasant for her even if you know the exercise helps her work off stress. Sadly, she's too big and ungainly to be able to play agility games all over the ship the way you do when you need to burn energy. You imagine you've seen parts of this ship she's never even imagined—although you think she might have helped design it, so you may be underestimating her.

At any rate, you're happy to let her enjoy you as she gently pedals. After all, just last night she snuck you cheese—even if it is processed for space travel—and has even tried to replicate catnip toys for you from medicinal herbs and fabric patches. She's told you stories of her cats, thinking you wouldn't understand, that you couldn't hear the joy in her voice when she told funny tales or the grief when she spoke of their passing.

It's possible you love her. Even though she doesn't comprehend what you are.

What any of your kind are.

Cats weren't the only ambassadors. But the others were killed off. The great leviathans and cetaceans. The pachyderms. The corvid. Even most of the primates are gone—except man, of course.

Your kind knew this die-off would happen. None of the others did what was needed to survive.

Adapt. Be accessible.

Move in. No, more than that: take over.

"That's enough for now. You want a ride to the cockpit?"

You chirrup and she laughs again, murmuring, "I swear you can understand me."

She strides down the corridors in the confident manner you love and her touch on your side is just right, respectfully light but keeping you secure as you bounce on her shoulder.

"Go get some chow," she tells Yashima, who gives you the slow eye blink of an experienced cat person.

You return it because you sense today is special.

She looks touched, as she should.

Once Yashima's left and Lassiter is in her seat, you jump onto the control panel, avoiding the touchpad to settle near the nav screen. You study it—and you imagine that to Lassiter, it just looks like so much scent-marking on your part—but you can see that the ship's headed in the right direction.

You purr just thinking about it.

Lassiter rubs around your ears as she looks at the display. "So much we don't know. What's out here? What does it all mean?"

These simple statements are why you're here. When the amount of people willing to admit they had much to learn finally far outnumbered the ones who allowed no room for questions, for wonder, for any answer but their own narrow beliefs, then you could act.

Then you could initiate contact on behalf of the planet you were seeded on.

And as you sit, you finally hear, with an ability the humans lack, the sound of The Seeders; it holds welcome and joy and even a tinge of surprise—did they think your kind couldn't do this?

Who but your kind could do this? You've always assumed it was why cats were sent—because world after world, you've wormed your way into not just the lives, but the hearts of the controlling species.

You've *domesticated* them.

Leaping onto Lassiter's chest, you make her hold you close, forcing her to abandon any other activity than petting you as you watch the progress of the ship and listen to the low psychic murmur of The Seeders. Their song of excitement and joy makes you happier than anything—except maybe the way this human touches you.

Her lips touch down on the fur of your neck, her breath soft. "Why do you always smell so good right there? Just one more mystery." She reaches out to the nav panel and makes a slight adjustment. "I'm scared and excited, Fluff. Some captain, huh? In awe of the unknown."

"Soon it will not be unknown," you say.

She hears it only as a purr.

For now.

ABOUT THE AUTHORS

Alice Dryden writes stories and poems about talking animals. Most of these are published in the furry fandom under the name Huskyteer, but occasionally one escapes into the wild. She is a motorcyclist who enjoys touring in Europe and believes all riders of two-wheeled vehicles should be nice to each other. Twitter: @ Huskyteer

•   •   •

Cherise Fong leads the life of a feral feline who shapeshifts into a human to ride her bicycle through the backstreets of Tokyo and across an archipelago of depopulated cat islands, enduring cedar ecologies, scarred infinity seawalls and forgotten insular communities, seeking out invisible stories and learning to read the air. Tweets @c4frog

•   •   •

Gerri Leen is a licensed cat wrangler (okay, the licensed part is made up) and shares her home with two feline overlords. She has many stories and poems published, including in *Nature*, *Escape Pod*, *Daily Science Fiction*, *Cast of Wonders*, and others. She's edited several anthologies for independent presses, is finishing some longer projects, and is a member of SFWA and HWA. See more at gerrileen.com.

•   •   •

Gretchin Lair is not as wise as Sage, asks as many questions as Whidbey, and is occasionally as stubborn as Shadow. She hates when dogs chase her while biking, especially in rural areas. If you contact her at gretchin@scarletstarstudios.com she would love to show you the photos she used as character references.

•　　　•　　　•

Jessie Kwak is a freelance writer and author of supernatural thriller *From Earth and Bone*, the *Bulari Saga* series of gangster sci-fi novels, and productivity guide *From Chaos to Creativity*. She lives in Portland with her husband, in a house overrun by bicycles and stacks of fabric. You can learn more about her at www.jessiekwak.com, or follow her on Twitter (@jkwak).

•　　　•　　　•

Judy Upton is an award-winning playwright and screenwriter. She's had short fiction published online and in magazines including: *Amsterdam Quarterly*, *Stonecrop Review*, *Penhelion*, *Hot Tub Astronaut*, *Suspense Magazine* and the novella *Maisie and Mrs Webster* by Orion Books. Her first novel, *What Maisie Didn't Know*, will be published by Wrecking Ball Press in 2021. Website: www.judyupton.co.uk

•　　　•　　　•

Juliet Wilson is an adult education tutor, conservation volunteer and crafter based in Edinburgh, United Kingdom. Her poetry and short stories have been widely published. She blogs at http://craftygreenpoet.blogspot.com and tweets @craftygreenpoet.

Kathleen Jowitt lives in Ely, works in London, cycles to the station, and writes on the train. She is the author of three novels and several short stories. You can find her at www.kathleenjowitt.com or @KathleenJowitt on Twitter, Facebook and Instagram.

.   .   .

Kiya Nicoll lives in an oak grove in New England with a number of cats who do not ride bicycles and a number of children who do. They write stories about people—or cats—on the edges and interstices of their worlds, who discover their realities are a little larger than they thought. "Like a Cat Needs a Bicycle" is one of the *Fog and Brass* steampunk fantasy stories, and several drabbles in the same world can be found at kiyanicoll.com.

.   .   .

Monique Cuillerier lives in Ottawa and writes near future science fiction. Her work has been published by *Diabolical Plots* and in the *Queer Sci Fi* anthologies, Impact and Migration. When not writing, she reads, knits, runs, gardens, and still manages to spend too much time on Twitter (@MoniqueAC) and not enough on her website (notwhereilive.ca).

.   .   .

Summer Jewel Keown lives in Indianapolis, Indiana, where she makes friends with all the cool neighborhood cats. Her short stories have been published in *Bikes Not Rockets*, *Pulp Literature*, *So It Goes*, and *Local Honey*. She has co-edited the fiction anthology *Non-stalgia*, and her romance novelist alter ego, Sofi Keren, has published the novels *Painted Over* and *False Starts & Artichoke Hearts*. Follow her on Twitter or Instagram @TheSummerJewel or on Facebook @SummerJewelKeown.